STRONG CURRENT EVOLUTION

STRONG CURRENT EVOLUTION

A Novel

Alexander D. Smith

iUniverse, Inc.
New York Bloomington Shanghai

STRONG CURRENT EVOLUTION

iUniverse books may be ordered through booksellers or by contacting:

iUniverse
1663 Liberty Drive
Bloomington, IN 47403
www.iuniverse.com
1-800-Authors (1-800-288-4677)

Because of the dynamic nature of the Internet, any Web addresses or links contained in this book may have changed since publication and may no longer be valid.

This is a work of fiction. All of the characters, names, incidents, organizations, and dialogue in this novel are either the products of the author's imagination or are used fictitiously.

ISBN: 978-0-595-49730-0 (pbk)
ISBN: 978-0-595-49438-5 (cloth)
ISBN: 978-0-595-61225-3 (ebk)

Printed in the United States of America

Acknowledgements

I want to acknowledge my lord and savior Jesus Christ for giving me the strength and the patience to write this book. Thank you for the breath that I breathe. I want to thank everyone who made this possible. To my wife for your support even though I may have acted like a butt. I owe you a lot more than I've given you. To my kids you get all the love in the world from me. I may not act like it but I will die for you. To my nieces I haven't forgotten about you. Towanda, Vivian, Helena, Latyeshia, Tatiana. You are my support. Anna, Theresa, Bob, Arthur, Letisia, you were my support system when I had none. To my dad, Alice, and Doris, you taught me some real stuff about life. I could never hate you for that. To all those who gave me the leisure time to write this book, much thanks goes out to you. You all know who you are. If you need to think about it, it probably isn't you.

Preface

I personally do believe a person can change. Sometimes things happen that are unforgettable. Sometimes someone close to us does them to us. Is It right to hate that person when whatever they did to us will slap them in the face several times. That's up to that individual to decide.

I feel that love conquers the worst hate, goodness conquers the most ill mannered feelings, and a true friend will tell you the truth even though it's a little bit hurtful. To be a true friend you hear what's said and if necessary use it. If you don't just throw it away. You don't have to use or listen to everything that someone says.

Beware though. Bad people come your way also and want you to follow. You have to stand up on your own two feet and take accountability because you are only one person. You will be that one person when you go to bed and when you wake up. You don't see two or three people when you look in the mirror.

Believe that you can do what you dream and of that dream has come true. I really do wish you luck in searching for the strength. It's there; all you have to do is find it. When you find it let it shine bright so others will see theirs more clearly.

Help someone find their light today.

SAME OLD THING

Since I found my dream girl my life has changed dramatically. I stay at the office more than I go on the road so my entertaining days are on hiatus. Let me explain this to you if you don't understand. My name is Mr. Smith. I own Smith Inc.

Smith Inc ... includes movie, theaters, trucking, distribution, advertising and much more. My favorites without question is record company (Black Dragon Records south Based in Atlanta), which my brother helped me establish before he died. We were broke before we got started so to have so much now is like a real dream. There is nothing in the world I take for granted.

I met Dottie in the hospital. She was a nurse or should I say "the nurse" who caught my eye. She also treated my injuries. The last thing I did for Lisa my (deceased wife) was trying to get her out of a bad situation. She had been kidnapped for ransom and was being held for 500,000 dollars. I had the money and was willing to pay. That's exactly what they were banking on.

I gathered up the money and was on the way to the old warehouse to make the exchange. I left the downtown New York (where my penthouse is) and headed upstate to the mansion. The morning was dark and gloomy kind of like my mood. I reached the main road that led to the house and slowed to let a cat pass me, and then ventured on.

The house sits on 22, 000 square feet including a personal gym, indoor and outdoor pool and basketball court called Shadyside Arena. What was a three-mile driveway is now one and a half for more parking spaces. The house itself is White with Blue shutters. As I pulled up to the entrance the gate opens automatically.

There are about ten cars in the driveway. They are probably my housekeepers (some who take up more of a permanent residence than others). Either way they do a good job so I don't complain. I pulled up to the last parking spot (my own personal) and kill the engine. I would normally take my time but there is none today. I grabbed the briefcase and headed up the stairs to the main hall.

I pass by the solid white pillars, which were made like the old palaces and into the main hall where in the middle sat a huge water foundation. Three angels were up top looking down at a figure of Jesus in the river getting baptized. I passed the foundation and headed to the family room. Everything in the room is White so it is a requirement that shoes be taken off before entering.

I walked into the room barefoot and headed past the canopy bed, the suede couch, the pearl color (custom made) television area and two-toilet bathroom to the far wall. I punched in a code on the revealed keypad and the giant portrait of my self slid to the left revealing a safe.

I emptied the contents of the briefcase into the safe and closed it back up. No I had to go upstairs to get the big bills (easier to carry). I took the elevator to the third floor and walked briskly to the end of the hall to the biggest bedroom. I opened the door and spotted my target. This is the room where I keep most of my money. Needless to say only I have access to this room.

I gathered the 500,000 dollars and left the room. It made me sick to think that someone would stoop to such low means to get money. I made one more stop into my room to shower and change clothes. I put down the briefcase and started the shower. I had over an hour to get there so I could slow down a little.

My only thoughts were (one) how could this happen (two) what was their actual plan and (three) I had to rescue her. I stepped out of the shower and dried off. I picked my black no nonsense suit with the gold cufflinks and big collar. The black alligators, tie and black shirt finished the job. I had no idea that I would be wearing red also.

I grabbed my keys and hustled down the stairs down to the main hall; no time for elevators. My bag was already downstairs and the fellas were out there too. I told them not to come but here they were anyway.

D, Bo, Art, and Shawn were standing by the truck. These are my homies. The guys that I grew up with are as loyal to me as I am to them.

"We heard what happened and knew that you would be here. After all the brawls, bar fights and everything you think we would let U do this alone. Lisa is like a sister to us so we all go or u don't".

I looked at Bo and asked "What's in the trunk? If you came all the way over here I know you have an idea".

I carried the suitcase to the truck and put it in the back.

"I think we shouldn't shoot our way in because we don't know where they are keeping her. I do think we should strap up so if they fire at us we won't be defenseless. I also think we should take two cars so she could be safe while we handle our business" I said.

I grabbed four guns with extra clips and the others did the same. I grabbed the suitcase and put it in the Porsche and told them follow behind me. I took off down the driveway and hit the main road. We had to go downtown past the penthouse to the old warehouse district. I hated doing it this way but I would give my life for her. She was very special to me.

Before I even realized we were almost there and I could see the warehouses. It looked abandon like most buildings on that side were. I slowed down and before long a man stepped out of the shadows and waved his hand to me. I pulled up and parked while the others stayed back. I could see them pull in as I was escorted into the warehouse.

The walls were decay red and there were freezers everywhere. I think it used to be a meat processing plant that moved to another building.

All the way at the other end of the floor I saw three men and a figure sitting down in a chair. I neared closer and saw it was her. I started running towards her with my heart going a mile a minute. I didn't recognize the men so I guess it must be random.

"Do you have the money" The leader asked?

"You all look gay in those suits" I replied.

"Don't make jokes or she gets it" He replied.

I started to laugh but saw he had a shotgun pointed to her head. It wasn't funny anymore.

"Ok (I replied) Let her go and you can have me instead plus keep the money".

I think he seemed to like the idea. He untied the ropes but then I heard her upstairs. It's a trick. I ran up the stairs to the office and kicked at the door. Finally, I pulled out the nine and fired two shots at the doorknob, Boom ... Boom. The door fell open and I kicked it the rest of the way. I shot the man behind the desk and untied her. Now what do I do.

The situation has changed. We're trapped in the upstairs office and they've started shooting at us. I told her to grab the suitcase and follow me. I leaned out of the office to see D, Bo, Art & Shawn blastin at these fools. I grabbed two guns and start into the action.

Now apparently they knew what was going to happen so they called extras. I started knocking then down and we reached the bottom of the stairs.

"Good to see ya" D said.

"Yeah right (I replied) let's get outta here".

Art said "Did you give them the money"?

I replied "NO".

"OK. Let's go" He replied.

We started to back up slowly and realized that we would have to run because I was on my last two guns and had two clips left. Everyone had reloaded. We had finally got shelter behind some boxes by the second door.

"We gotta run for it" I said to Lisa.

We got up to run when I saw Lisa was being pulled back. I ran up to the guy, put my gun to his brain and blew it away. I grabbed her hand and we started to run. I grabbed the suitcase and we caught up faster to the rest of the crew. We're almost to the door. D, Bo, Art, Shawn were at the truck.

I saw Art reaching for the semi-automatic. I stopped and saw her on the ground not moving. I picked her up and started to run to the truck. Money in one hand her on my shoulder I was there, I saw it. Boom … Boom … Boom … Boom … Boom.

The men who shot me were going down but I was hit five times. I lay there holding her in my arms as if I wasn't hurt. My suit was red but I didn't care. I had one shot left and if I had any strength left in me I would use it.

The leader came out alone. He was hit but not bad I would fix that. He leaned over me and said something but I didn't hear it. He leaned closer and said it so he knew I heard him. He put his gun on my head and said "Rot in hell" as he pulled back the trigger.

I heard a shot and he fell on the ground. I had shot him instead of his shooting me. I thought I was dead. I just lay there thinking we will be alright my baby and me. Everything will be just fine.

I woke up in the hospital three days later. It was all over the news on how I got shoot. They said wrong place at the wrong time. I am so glad they said that. I should be up for murder but my PR had to make something up because she didn't know what happened. Then the other part of the story came up and I found out the Lisa was dead. I had promised that I would never cry for anyone but the floodgates opened and it was hella hard to close them.

By the time my boys got there they could see I had found out. They told me how I killed the leader and carried Lisa to the truck along with the money, before I passed out. She had been shot seventeen times so to avoid having to see it they had her cremated. I think that was a good move because I would have done the same thing. They showed me the urn and for obvious reasons I couldn't touch it.

Bo came up to me and said he couldn't touch it either. "Just not ready to say goodbye yet. Before she died she came to and told you that she loved you and for you to move on. I drove your car back to the house with the money. So no one knows anything about it".

Art who is usually the strong one was crying like a little baby. Shawn who always talks too much wasn't saying a word. Lisa's mother who came to see me was holding the urn. She leaned over and kissed me on my forehead. My vision was starting to clear and I could see that the room was full of flowers and cards.

"My daughter was so happy while she was with you. She loved having us over every weekend and the cookouts, and parties. To share you with us was her biggest joy. She started to let out tears. She went the way she wanted to go; right beside you. I do and always will love you like a mother loves a son. I will be back later with the rest of the family. We are staying at her house so come by when U get better". Then she grabbed the Urn and darted out of the room.

I had many more visitors during the three months in the hospital. My three children came to visit along with my in laws. Most of all I enjoyed Dottie's company. Let me tell U why.

DOTTIE

I had three nurses per day for the first month. They mostly wanted to be my nurse because of who I was. They also wanted to find out my story so that they could make some money with the tabloids. My kids who are all grown now have come to see me very often and in effect are making me home sick. I have had the thought that they (the nurses) are trying to get in my good graces so they can sleep with me later.

That's where Dottie comes in. Dottie replaced Catherine, Rachel & Rene. Where they fumbled the ball she excelled. Where they a good job she did a great one. Where they had no experience she was da bomb. Plus she was so much nicer and her figure was to die for. Baby had back.

Catherine was a little on the shy side. She worked the nightshift and said she wanted to suck me off. I kept her at bay by asking about her family. She loved to talk about her family. She loved her family as much as she loved me. For her to nurse me back to health was a dream come true for her. Her dream was to become a back up dancer and buy her folks a house. She was a thin girl with a models body. She wasn't that cute but had that baby face you just can't deny.

She admitted to me that even though she was a freak and likes to be spanked, that she had to know you a little before she let you do it. She went to Harvard and got her Bachelors degree in business before she got her RNC (Registered Nurse) degree. She weighed about one hundred eighty pounds and had ankles like a dancer although she hadn't taken a class. She tried to be funny but couldn't tell jokes.

Her father died in the war so her mother raised her the best way she could. From the looks of it she did a good job. She lived in the Bronx and had a different boyfriend every week; so no one knew how freaky she really was. Her current boyfriend wanted to meet me so bad he got fired for leaving work early. I made a phone call and got his boss to give him his job back.

She said she couldn't be my nurse anymore because she was having fantasies about me and couldn't do her job properly. So Dottie came in and replaced her for the nightshirt. Rachel and Rene used to hang with cat (Catherine) so they were kind of pissed when she left.

Rachel was flamboyant, full of energy, a ball of kinetic energy. She wasn't shy at all. I didn't mess with her like that because if she told, she would get fired and I would get moved. She was five-seven, one hundred fifty pounds. She was real pretty but had an ugly attitude, which made her unattractive. She loved dollars and thugs. Both of which I possessed. I lived the lifestyle she wanted so she clung to me.

All she talked about was herself, her dreams, her life, her, her, her, her, shit. Why would I want to get involved with someone like that? I was like that once. I saw myself in a woman's body and I hated that. I wish I could take back every bad thing I ever did to a woman.

Her father was still in her life, but she never talked to him. She treated her mother the same way. They sent her to a summer camp three years in a row and she never forgave them for it. She left the house at the age of eighteen and never looked back. They reach out to her but she doesn't respond. All she said is why they this and why they that.

So I asked for her to be replaced and Dottie liked me so much that she took that shift. So now Rene is feeling the pressure big time and is starting to act out. I do feel sorry for her but I have to be comfortable. Needless to say things went down hill with Rene.

Rene used to be one of the funniest people I know. Now she sees how Rachel looks at me and reacts the same way. If I was in her position I would be worried about myself. So I did her a favor and sent her to another patient so to speak. I asked for a full time nurse and Dottie came forward. Now I was still grieving over the loss of Lisa so it was perfect timing.

Rene was a time bomb that exploded. Her five-seven, one hundred fifty frame, cute faced self, came into my room and started cursing at me and had to be restrained, by hospital staff, and security. No ... wrong incident ... that was a different one. Dottie had to let loose on her a couple times. One time she knocked Rene out cold. I was glad she was there.

I had a talk with Dottie. One day when she came into my room and I asked her a couple questions.

"What's going on Mr. Smith? Are u feeling ok? Is there anything you need"?

"We'll there is actually something I need to ask you while you're here Dottie" I replied.

A smile crept across her face. She loved when I said her name. She said it made her feel like she was important. Now that I had her attention it would be easy to ask my questions.

Dot, I know we talked about your family and everything, and I've told you about mine. Tell me do you have a husband or boyfriend or something or someone of that nature" I asked her?

"No I don't Mr. Smith. I do have to question your motives though" she said jokingly.

"Well, First of all you can call me Devonte. I was wondering because I am getting out of the hospital and I need a full time nurse to stay at my home until I get better. I was just wondering if you were interested. It would only be for two or three months" I said.

"Well I would have no problem except I'm moving back to Atlanta at the end of the week. Other than that I would say yes" She looked upset.

"Why are you upset" I asked?

"For one I would like to get to know you better because I think you're cute. Two, I could start my own business and three I do want to make sure you get better" she said.

"Really" I asked?

"Yes really" she said.

"OK. If I moved to my house in Atlanta would you do it then? You could stay with me. I have plenty of room. What do you think"?

"I would love to (she shouted). This is going to be so much fun I can't wait".

"So why are you waiting until the end of the week. Why not leave today or tomorrow? What's stopping you"?

"I could leave early like Wednesday and transfer to Atlanta General Hospital. I could do it that way. What I was really trying to do was leave all together" she replied.

"You could leave from that hospital. Use your Bachelors and Master degrees to start your own business. Make your own money, hours, and schedule that way they can't stop you from doing anything" I replied.

"Are you ready to get out of here or are you going to wait" She asked?

"Let's go" I said.

Without hesitation I called the fellas and told them what was going on. They were there within thirty minutes of me hanging up the phone.

(Mr. Smith) The administrator called as Dottie pushed my wheelchair down the hallway." You're leaving the hospital. I see on your chart you still have two to three months of recovery. So you're going to rehab at home huh? If something were to go wrong that you would need to go to the hospital it may be too late".

"Mr. Blake, I'm going home to get some relaxation and rest. I may have sex while I'm there but you won't be there to tell me shit. Now goodbye" I said.

Shawn was honking the horn when we came out. "Come on we gotta go now" He yelled!!!

Dottie pushed the chair up to the car and I used the doorframe to push myself in the car. She told Shawn to wait until she pulled up behind us so she could follow us. She didn't take the long and we were out of there in no time.

"So where is your stuff" I asked?

I already sent it there" she replied.

When we arrived at the house the wheelchair was waiting for me at the front door. She was surprised by how I lived. I never thought of building a ramp to the front door. Right about now I'm glad Lisa did. I entered the foyer and came to a stop at the statue. I began to push myself into the front room when I heard SUR-PRISE!!!

Everyone was there to welcome me home. My kids, Lisa's family and even more amazing Dottie's folks were there. Normally I wouldn't be surprised but being in a hospital room around flowers kind of dulled my senses. Her (Dottie) relatives came up to me and expressed their sympathy for my loss. I thought that I would really miss her and not be able to look at another woman again.

Dottie had told them something about me. Needless to say they read between the lines and put two and two together. I wasn't ready for that and she knew it; but I couldn't make her stop feeling the way she felt. For some odd reason I kind of felt the same way. It's not the same love … its different love and I realize that. I still had to get better first.

The food was on the grill and the music was playing. Dot's relatives came up here to take her home. She spent so much time at the hospital that they started spending time downtown. They ran into my people and exchanged numbers. So when my boys called and told them what's happening they came over to the house. They surprised her too but she still wanted to see the house.

My next thought (I'm glad I put in the elevator) was erased when she touched my hand. I was showing her around the different rooms and she was amused by the way they were decorated. Then I showed her the white room. She flips out and before I knew it she took her shoes off and moved over to a silver briefcase that should have had blood all over it. She rubbed her hand against it and looked back at me.

The look on my face told her a lot. I didn't know but she was not the only one I was leading on this tour. So while she put back on her shoes D, Shawn, Bo, and Art were showing the house. I asked her to grab the case and hand it to me. We waited for everyone else to go back downstairs and I showed the rest of the house.

After I told her what actually happened to put me in the hospital she started to cry. I told her that it was not her fault. That she had nothing to be sorry about. That would be our secret. Except for my folks and her nobody knew and nobody would.

I left the briefcase in the money room and started to go downstairs.

"I don't know why I feel for you the way I do. It's the feeling when you know it is something good…. something that you don't want to give away. Do you know what I mean" She asked?

"Yeah I do" I replied.

We returned back downstairs and were each greeted with a plate of food. Grandpa was cooking because I couldn't. One thing about him he could cook his ass off. When she walked over to the table I saw her true beauty. Her dark skin coinciding with her curves and her round hips made me want to scream. She was a thick girl. I love them thick. More cushion for the pushing.

It was getting close to clean up now. It's around nine o'clock and I'm restless. I wanna get out of this chair and walk around. The depression is starting to get to me. Usually Lisa would be here beside me and I wouldn't be lonely. I just sat in the corner looking out of the window. No one will find me … this house is too big. There are too many rooms.

Just that quick in all the rooms of the house she walks into the one I'm in. What luck, how did she know? Did someone tell her?

"I thought you would be in here, come on downstairs" she said.

"I'll be down in a minute. I need sometime alone. I need to think" I said.

"You don't need to be alone right now. You need your friends. We will all help you. I'll take you downstairs" she said.

"OK" I replied.

She was right the last thing I needed was to be alone. I needed to be around people to keep my mind in the present. I grieved for a month but it still hurts. I looked at the suitcase and I just wanna shoot holes in it. I can't stop the pain. I want to stop it but it's impossible.

I had to get myself together. I have a family to support, still I couldn't help wonder what Lisa would have done if she had lived, and I had died. Would it be different? Would she ever be the same again? Tonya my assistant asked me was I alright. A tight look of concern spread over her face as if she wanted me to ask what was wrong.

"What's wrong" I asked?

"The doctor's on the phone for you" she said.

"Really what did he have to say" I asked?

"He wants to tell you personally" she said.

I pushed myself into the room and picked up the phone.

"What's up Doc" I said?

"You are going to have to be in the chair for a little while longer" He said.

"How long all together" I asked?

"Six months" He said.

"What ever is necessary for me to get better? But one question Doc. Can I take a plane ride or is it too early" I asked?

"If you feel you're up to it but be careful. I would not advise it but you are going to do what you are going to do anyway. For my own curiosity why would you want to take a plane" He asked?

"Just asking "I said smiling.

CHANGE OF PACE

As many plane rides as I have taken in my life, they have never been this hard. We've been here for two months and a half of my recovery is complete. If I knew it was going to be like this I would have saved that last bullet for me instead of him. It feels like solitary confinement. The good news is I am distancing my feeling from Lisa. I know she is still watching me.

I finally have the privacy I need to get things together. Dottie stays here at the house so she is on call but she only does medical things so she gets more rest than she used too. She is even looking better than she used to. Atlanta is not as busy as New York but it is still jumping. She has a lot more time now so she runs for an hour or two everyday. My estate is so huge that she doesn't have to leave the property.

My estate sits on fifty thousand acres. The driveway runs all the way to the main house with buildings on either side all the way down. The studio and housekeepers quarters are on either side closest to the house. The blue brick building on the left houses maids, servants, the butler etc ... while the black and red building on the right is the studio. The dragon surrounded in fire on the wall identifies the entrance.

The main hall separates into three areas Studio A, (on the left) Studio B (on the right) and my personal studio upstairs. The black carpet and red walls unfold through out the entire building. All of my plaques line the walls that lead to the kitchen, billiard room and pressroom. The billiard table is blue with clear balls. I had the dragon put inside the balls and the numbers encased in black on the sides. I also put the emblem on the sticks so can't anybody steal them.

The kitchen is state of art. Since a lot of time is spent there I had to give it that home feel. There's no place like home right. The house is the same way but without the fountain. Instead I had my artist of the year and my lifetime achievement awards blown up and embedded into the floor. The spiral steps (which started on both sides) led upstairs, but it you go straight back through the living room you could catch the platinum elevator.

If I start to go broke that's the first thing I'm selling. My cars were parked downstairs in the basement. I built a ramp so I could get them out easier than before. The loveliest things about the garage (basement) are the cars. All of them custom made.

The living room furnished with blue suede carpet and white furniture is my favorite room. Six recliners enclosed around a couch (suede). The flat screen is hooked up to my surround sound audio system. Duplicate plaques are all over the house. Right behind the TV room to the right of the Billiard room (same kind of balls) is the theater.

The theater seats seventy people, has a custom-made hundred-inch screen. I also have it designed where my emblem comes up on the screen when you turn it on or off. I found out it's not about how much money you have, but how much fun you have. I spend most of my time in here, the living room or bedroom.

All the bedrooms in the house are the same except my bedroom. Imagine Richie Rich grown up. All the other rooms have the white walls, black and red carpet and the huge white canopy bed and a huge bedroom. Better than the best hotel suite you have ever seen. My room had blue carpeting that seems to connect with the walls. The sea blue paint starts from the bottom and goes up to the ceiling. If you are drunk, do not come into this room.

My viewing area is like the one in the front room but is enclosed in a blue entertainment center. With just one of my speakers I can blow all your windows out. All the windows are double paned so nothing breaks. This is where I loss myself. Separate myself from the rest of the world. Find myself all over again when I am lost. I am looking out of the window when the door opens.

A picture next to me catches my attention…. Lisa and I together. This is the only picture or article I have pertaining to her at this house. All her stuff in New York was given to her parents along with some money and the house we brought together. There are too many memories. All I really need is this one.

As I'm holding this picture I remember faintly her voice. We were in the car on the way to the hospital and my eyes are open. I kept telling her to hold on. Not to give up and hold on we can make it. She opened her eyes and said "I'll be yours forever take me with you and I'll live forever. I love you; always will…. But move on. Then she closed her eyes and she was gone. Someone touched me and I almost jumped out of the chair. Maybe death at last was here.

It was Dottie.

"Scared you a little huh" she asked?

"Ha … Ha … Ha … very funny" I replied.

She picked the picture up and looked at it. She sat down on the bed and started to stare out of the same window I was.

"You really do miss her huh. She must have been a wonderful woman. How long were you together? I lost someone special to me too. We were in separable. He went on a trip and was found dead in his cabin. We were married for three weeks but we were together for ten years. I never thought to loss someone would hurt so much. That was three months ago when I started working at the hospital".

I looked at her and she looked back at me. I saw tears start to fall from her eyes. I got up out of the chair and joined her on the bed. I held her as tightly as I could.

"I never told anyone that … Be … Before. I figured that if I held it in that it would go away. Now it's just tearing me apart. It helps to be around people because I don't have to think about it you know" she said.

"I know exactly what you mean" I replied.

A smile crept over her face.

In no time at all I was walking around. I spent a lot of the time in the studio (my second home). I haven't come out with a record in years even though I used to sleep in the studio. It was always for someone else. Millions of hits to my credit and I was now feeling an urge to get back out there. I could put out an album tomorrow but my artists come first. I have a lot to say and I need to say it but if I do this it is not only me involved.

I called Bo and D into the room. They were busy but they came anyway. I had to really get this off my chest. Never have I called them into the studio so they knew it must be important. Fortunately Art and Shawn were there so they came to. I sat them all down.

"I have to call a meeting with all the artists. I always try to put them first but this time I have to do something for me. I'm putting together an album that I'm going to put out if they don't like it or want to leave then that's that. What I have to say will be heard. I'm working on tracks now but I can't do vocals until I'm fully healed. So get in touch with everyone because I'm recording in three months" I said.

Art spoke up first "It seems as though you already made your decision. We'll start calling people and tell them to come as soon as possible. Everything is going to be fine".

For the first time since the accident I felt enthusiastic about anything. I ran the idea by Dot and she agreed with me.

"I think it's a wonderful idea. I would love to be on it. It might even help me get better myself. When are you going to start it? Let me know OK", she said excitedly.

I took a shower and changed clothes. She checked my bandages every now and then but mostly we just talked. It seemed like we had known each other since forever. The more we talked the more we had in common. We started to workout together. We would take long walks and talk about my plans and her plans. We even passed along the possibility of us two getting together.

I could see myself with her. She's smart, sexy, straightforward, kind, and funny. I don't know where it's going to stop but I am enjoying the ride. I wasn't using the chair anymore and my weight was picking back up. Things were looking up. The word got around about the album and everyone started to pop up. Pretty soon the whole house was full. All fifty people got comfortable in the theater.

"You all probably know why I called you. I know you heard the word. How the radio station found out about it I don't know. I do know this much. This album is going to touch a lot of people" I said.

There was no response. No one said a thing. I knew that they would not really be receptive to the idea but somebody could have said something. Finally Curtis (smooth) spoke up.

"I think it's not a bad idea. I had the last album to come out and it's been a while since we've heard something from you. Here and there stuff is good but people need something they can listen to. Something that gets them moving when they can't" He replied.

It felt good to have all of their support. The same way I gave them.... they gave me. I was up on a cloud and I wasn't coming down anytime soon. I left the room like everything was going to be alright. That was until Patricia said that she had something to say.

Everyone was shocked. Since they've been here (at the company) they respected my decisions and I respected theirs. If they had a problem they could always come and talk to me and vice versa. So why would she have something to say to me after the meeting was over and not during. I was visibly upset by this, as was everybody else.

Chris was the one to speak up for the group.

"I think that it's a great idea and you do have your opinion but don't think that ..." He started to say.

"Now come on let her say what she has to say" I said interrupting him.

"Well, she said pulling her shirt down below her waist line. I don't think it's a good idea. Actually it sucks. My album ... My first album is supposed to come out next month. I think that should be the way it is. It's not about you Mr. Smith, it's about me Patricia Boggs. It's my turn and I will not be denied" She said.

I promised my doctor I would take it easy. I'm trying to figure out how this not nothing yet-wanna be something artist is going to tell me what I'm going to do. Who does she think she is? I should slap the taste out of her mouth. If my doctor was here now he would be saying (calm down do not over exert yourself).

On top of that Dottie was giving me the look I knew she had but didn't want to see. I threw my hands up to say I understand.

"First of all let's get one thing straight. I own this record company you don't. I make the moves that are best for this company. The reason you came to this label is because of reputation. The reputation I along with my brother created and I plus the people in front of you uphold. So for you to talk to me like that means you have no respect at all for this staff, your fellow artists or me. Now that I said that, if you still fell the same way you don't have to even be here compendia" I said.

As soon as she opened it her mouth was closed. Just when I thought she was finished she started up again.

"OK (she said) you got that one. I would get all up in my feelings if my husband died and it was my entire fault. Don't take your pain out on me you called the dumb meeting and wanted to get this out in the open so huh. It's all in the open" She screamed!!!

Now I was pissed. No one had ever seen me like this. This bitch does not have the right to talk about my shit. I'm going to kick her ass all the way back to New fucking York. She does not know what is going to happen. Dot is just looking at me puzzled. I don't care how much pain I'm in this bitch is going to get it.

Before anyone could react I was right in front of her. She tried to back up but there was nowhere to run. Fear spread in here eyes and she tried unsuccessfully to get around me. She started to breath heavily. Now before I met Lisa this girl wouldn't even be standing this long. I think she would have pissed on herself but she was too scared.

"I could have threatened to hurt your people too but I know something you don't think I do. You don't have an album to put out because every producer is either too hard for you or you don't want to fucking work. You're late for the studio and want someone else's time. This business doesn't work like that. My wife's death was not my fault and I could kill you for saying that but I'm going to do you a really big favor and me at the same time. YOU'RE FIRED. You didn't hear me YOU'RE FIRED. Get out of my house and if you ever come back to the studio it will be considered trespassing" I said.

Her body slipped onto the floor. Bodyguards picked her up and put her out. I watched on the computer as they drove her to the front gate, let her out and watched it close behind her. The look on her face was identical to a balloon being popped. I'm not going to lie ... that hurt.

Dottie came over and touched me to get my attention. The ringing in my ears must have been her calling my name because it got louder as she came towards me. I looked at her and she could see the pain in my eyes. I felt like falling to the floor in the spot.

"I really think you need to rest. It's been a long day and you look exhausted" Dottie said.

She led me to the elevator and pressed three. When we arrived at the room she told me to lie down on the bed. My shirt was covered with blood. Everyone else saw it but I didn't. She cleaned my wounds and put on new bandages.

"As long as you rest it will be just fine. I'm glad you didn't hit her. That would have been a lawsuit and you don't need that" She said.

"I know I gottta get better so this album can come together. I got the tracks all I need are the vocals. Give me two months. I'll be ready" I said.

WORKING IT OUT

Six months have passed and I'm completely healed. I headed downtown and received a standing ovation on every floor. I walked into the meeting in progress and almost instantly Arnold stopped. I ushered for him to continue and at that moment I understood why marketing was up five percent. After the meeting adjourned we spoke about progress.

See Arnold is Lisa's brother. He took over where she left off and carried the ball. Arnold was a big guy. Six two; two-forty (down from two eighty). We became best friends before I knew that was Lisa's brother. He got an assistants job on his own but inherited the director's job. I didn't mind because I promoted him. He started the conversation first.

"How are you" He asked?

"I'm doing great man" I replied.

"No, I mean how are you doing" He asked?

"Well, I'm getting along" I replied.

"I miss that girl to def man" he said.

"Yeah I do to" I replied.

"So what happened because no on ever told me" He asked?

"Let's go in my office I'll tell you all about it" I said.

We walked into my office and I shut the door. I began to tell him about the whole thing. I even told him what Patricia said.

"She got like that on you dog? Now personally I would have knocked her ass out. You did the right thing though. The last thing you need is a lawsuit. I know how that shit is … in and out of court and you really can't go anywhere. Kind of like that wheelchair huh? I don't know how u did it. I would have gone crazy. So what's up with Dottie? Do u think that there is a future in that? I would go for it. She would want for you to be someone strong. So what's happening now" He asked?

"It's time to go back to what I love doing. My first love is music so I'm going to make an album. I feel like I'm strong enough to do it, plus I have everyone's support. I already got some tracks made now I only gotta put down vocals. Dot says she's interested in singing on the album. She has a very beautiful voice you should hear her" I replied.

"You speak very fondly of her. Are you hooked up with her yet? I met her at the barbeque. She looks good. I would date her myself but she was all over you. She looks like she wants you. What you gonna do about that" He asked?

"I want to get with her but she lost somebody too. So I don't know if she wants to make that move. I'm going to have to see because I really do like her. So we will see what happens" I responded.

"Yeah let's see" he said.

I was surprised that my office had not changed a bit. I still had a picture of Lisa on my desk; I couldn't take my eyes off of it. My desk was always clean. The only difference was the brown leather couch was moved to the opposite side. The chairs were in the same place.

Arnold put his hand on the picture and put it face down on the desk. "She knows how you feel about her. You can't hide your feelings you don't have to. You know what? (He stood up and came over to my side of the desk). The next time I see you two you all better be a couple".

My secretary beeped "You have a visitor Mr. Smith".

"OK send them in" I replied.

Dottie walked in and gave me a kiss on the cheek. I was kind of shocked but didn't show it.

"I need to talk to u" She whispered.

Arnold looked at me, then her, then me, then her, and then said, "Remember what I said".

He got up and left the office shutting the door behind him. He looks through the window and shoots me a look. I waved him off, got up and shut the blinds. I locked the door and walked over to her. There was something in her eyes that I couldn't explain. It turned me on and I responded.

I walked over to her, put my lips upon hers and waited to see if she would kiss me back. Almost instantly she returned the reaction and before long we were all over each other. We moved simultaneously over to the couch and she fell on top of me. I never thought about this happening but apparently she had. She knew what she wanted to do. So I let her have her way with me.

She began to strip off my clothes slowly purposely taking her time. First my shirt and then my pants came off. She giggled when she realized my boxers had my name on them. She had worn a skirt so that all she had to do was pull it up. She climbed on top of me and let herself go. I think she hit an all-new level before she started to climax. Before we finished I was pounding her pussy so hard she was reaching for the windows. She said my name and let out a sigh as we climate simultaneously.

I put back on my clothes and looked at her eagerly.

"So this means we hook' in up right" I asked?

"I really would like to be" she replied.

"So when in Rome do as the Romans do. I want to be with U, you want to be with me so I guess we are a couple (I said) so I will see you tonight in my special place. So don't make any plans. I am in control. Tonight your body is calling and I am picking up the phone" I replied.

"Ok Mr. Smith" She said smiling.

Tonight was on. I mean it's going to be special. I picked up some scented candles, flowers and some massage oils. First thing I did once I got home was clean. The house itself was clean but the room I was using wasn't. I put clean linen on the bed. I put candles all around the room. The massage table was ready to go and the steam room was burning up.

I had an idea of how she was going to take this. This is my plan to get her into my bed (which it was) but why be so obvious. So I had an idea. We would have a picnic and eat first. So I finished setting up in the room. I had many plans that I wanted to accomplish. I wanted to make her orgasm before we even had sex.

I laid down a tablecloth over the large table and put in a movie. I'm not sure which one I picked but I remembered one that made me cry once. Then I headed downstairs and started to cook. I made it to the kitchen before anyone else got there so I got to work. I started to boil my water for the spaghetti, chopped up some onions and sausage.

I could tell she would like that because she loved everything accept hot peppers, (which I don't either). I diced some mushrooms and green peppers and threw them in with the mixture of onions and sausage. I opened up the back door so the air could come in. I also made garlic bread. So the only thing left was the shrimp and the choice of wine.

After I pulled the cake out of the oven and set it on the stove, I put on the lobster. It was about four o' clock now. Everything should be finished by five. She would be home by six and that's when the festivities would start. I decided to make some fish so I wouldn't mess up my appetite.

I pulled up to the large brown building and jumped out of the car. My blue suit caught the eye of several nurses in the parking lot. Dottie had started her own clinic and had so many clients she had to move to a building bigger than she ever thought she would have. The main lobby looked a lot like a hospital with a homier feel to it.

I pushed the button to go to the top floor when a group of teenagers stopped me.

"Ewe.... Do you know who you are? I mean do you know who I am; I mean is it really you here, now? Pinch me girl I must be dreaming" One of them said.

"Yes it's me. What can I do for you ladies" I asked?

The oldest one pulled put a notepad and asked for my autograph. I started to sign several autographs.

"Girl my mom is not going to believe this. Sign this one to Delores good luck from Mr. Smith". If only she were here right now. Can we get some pictures" She asked me?

It's been a while since I've been in the limelight so I didn't mind at all, plus it was only five-twenty. I had a little bit of time to kill. I posed for several pictures then headed up to the fifth floor. I poked my head out of the elevator and stepped off gingerly. I felt fine but I still had to be careful.

I walked up to the receptionist desk and asked the young lady to call the director for me. That's the title Dottie took when she started the clinic. The young lady was still talking on the phone while the other nurses passing by were trying to get her attention. While she was still talking on the phone I signed a few autographs.

I saw Dottie and walked back to her office. The receptionist at the desk had turned around and nearly fell out of her chair when she realized she ignored me. She ran to catch up with me but the door was closed before she got there.

"I get off in five minutes. I can't stand that girl. She gets on my nerves. All she does is talk on the phone. I want to replace her but I don't have anyone else. She looked at me wide eyed. Do you know someone that could replace her? If you do call them for me" Dottie asked me?

"We will deal with that tomorrow but right now we are leaving. You didn't tell them that you were dating me. Did you tell them that you even knew me" I asked?

"No ... I wanted to earn the respect that I have now don't be mad at me" she pleaded.

"I can't be mad at you. I think it's better to earn respect than have it handed to you. Plus they would have been asking for favors. You know parties and things like that. I'm glad you didn't tell anyone; but now that they do know me they will start asking questions. If you wanna ask me you can if not tell them no. Work is work and play is play. I know you can handle it" I replied.

We walked out of the office and the same one that I couldn't get off the phone was already gone. Dottie gave me that look as if to reiterate what she said. I nodded in approval and we caught the elevator as it came up. When we got to the ground floor the building was almost empty. Security was behind the desk looking at camera or so I thought. I stood in front of the camera for two minutes and he never looked up.

The employees clambering up in the lobby were looking and pointing. Finally one female came up and asked the question that every one wanted answered. Gingerly she walked up and asked" are you …

"Yes" I replied.

"I told you all" she said.

Many of the women that came over wanted to say thank you and to ask for an autograph. (These are the people who will buy my next album) I thought as I signed a few autographs. I began to walk outside and Dottie joined me.

"Sorry about that some last minute business that had to be taken care of. I promise there will be no more interruptions" she said.

"I know (I replied) because we are leaving right now" I said.

The ride home was not bad at all the only thing was she wanted to know what I had planned for her. I wanted to tell her but I wanted to show her more. I pulled into parking area and shut off the engine. The car itself seemed to slide into the parking spot by itself. She got out of the car and came to the bottom of the stairs.

"I'm not coming up until you tell me" she screamed!!!

I kept walking up the stairs and she ran behind me.

"I ran you a bath in the room. Go get in and I'll be up in a minute. That's all I'm going to tell you for now, but you have to promise to do everything I say without questions ok" I asked?

"OK … I promise" she replied.

I instructed the Butler to bring the food up to the room around seven. I wasn't sure if she likes Lobster or Fish but she didn't have to eat it if she didn't like. I went into the bedroom and undressed. I slipped into the water without her noticing.

I began slowly to wash her body. She hadn't been touched in a while because I found her spots immediately. My hand was a magnet and it was picking up everything. Now that she was clean it was her turn to wash me up. She did not use the rag. She used the soap and her hand. She knew what to do. She did not touch the usual parts but everything else was up for grabs.

I had to stop because if I didn't the whole evening would be ruined. I grabbed her hands and brought her close to me. I whispered in her ear "get out and dry off". She did this with no problem. After I let the water out I put on my robe. She had on hers with her Bra and a pair of thongs.

If I ripped into her now she wouldn't care, but I had to preserve the evening. Seven o'clock there was a knock on the door. I had forgotten that I told the Butler to bring the food up. I pulled my seat up; the Butler began to prepare the meal. The aroma of Lobster and Spaghetti filled the air and she just smiled.

We ate in silence, enjoying each other's company. I fed of her vibes and she fed off mine. She knew I wanted her but it just wasn't time. If I say so the food was delicious and she agreed getting a second helping.

"Now that was delicious. Did you cook" she asked?

"Actually I did cook. I'm glad you liked it" I said.

I rose up from the table and grabbed her hand. She stood up and drew herself close to me. As our lips touched our souls ignited and became one. The only things on our minds were each other and that's all that mattered. I broke the seal our lips had created and while her eyes were still closed I tied a blindfold around her eyes. I sat her back down in the chair and told her to wait five minutes.

I could tell that she was enjoying the evening and her body showed me. It won't be long now. Fuck the movie I want her ASAP. I lit all of the candles in the room and turned on the sauna. The massage table was ready and the main event was coming up.

I went back into the other room, grabbed her hand and led her to the massage table. I laid her down on the table and watched as the oils sunk into her skin. Her body relaxed to the point that every time I touched it; it was calling out for me.

I wanted her right now, but this had to last. It's been too long to rush it. We will have plenty of time for the quick stuff. Tonight is special. If I don't do this right it could blow everything. I'll take my time and her body will tell me when it's time to go.

She turned over on her back so now her chest was facing me. Personally I don't know how long I could hold on myself. My hands were moving by themselves now. They had minds of their own and she loved every bit of it. I could tell that she was about to climax so I stopped for a minute. Then I lifted her up off the table and slipped and towel around her, then I slipped one around myself.

It was sauna and candles. I took off the blindfolds and the heat in her eyes told me NOW NOW NOW!!! I pulled her into the sauna and before I knew what happened the dam broke and the dogs were out. We were all over each other and a hurricane could not stop us. My body was hers and hers was mine, one complete unit. The heat from the steam room made it more intense and before long she found JR. She sucked me so hard I wanted to scream. The grand finale was here and finish line was near.

Expolsive Situation

Somehow we ended up on the floor and made our way out of the sauna. Our bodies were drenched in each others scent and sweat. S he fucked me and I fucked her. She exploded on top of me and I cam only seconds later.

Our bodies were still hot for each other. I lifted her up and carried her to the bed. The fire in her eyes was still burning and I had to put that fire out. As soon as we looked in each other's eyes it was body against body. Like a train with no breaks we were moving against each other. I became her, she became me.

"Damn ... this shit is good" I said.

"I want you to fuck me like I'm leaving tomorrow" She screamed!!!

That only made me drive harder and harder. She had lost control and she loved it. She's on top of me and I'm on top of her. It seemed like forever was upon us and we passed it by and kept going. I felt like I was going to bust.

"Slow down" I said.

"I don't know if I can" she moaned.

"Fuck it" I said.

I turned her over and started to hit her from behind. I was my destiny to give her what she wanted.

Fuck me ... Fuck me ... Oh shit ... Fuck me damn it ... AAAAHHHH!!!! I'm Cumming" she screamed.

"AAAAHHHH shit I'm Cumming too" I screamed!!!

"That was amazing. I have never felt that before. We need to do that again sometime soon" She replied.

As she lay there in my arms I held her closely. I knew that for the time being that fire was put out. I also knew that it could rise up again at any minute. This is what I wanted … to satisfy her to the point her sexual hunger was fulfilled.

I feel like I can do anything with her. That nothing is off limits. I am a part of her now and she is part of me. As long as I live I will remember tonight.

"Are you ready for round three then" I asked?

"Huh" She asked?

Before she could answer I was all over her and she knew what was going on. I'm not even sure we went to sleep that night. All I could tell you is that pussy will be on my mind for a while.

Since things were cool at the office I was spending a lot of personal time in the studio. Almost all of the tracks were completed and the verses were written. All I had to do was put them down on tape. I was working on this track called "loved and lost" when the bell at the gate rang.

Now everyone who is allowed knows the code because it never changes. I flicked the video camera and it was Patricia Boggs. I don't know what she was doing back here but I wasn't letting her in. It wouldn't hurt to hear her out though, would it … Probably not?

Chris came in and said "Patricia is at the gate. Should I let her in"?

"Go ahead open the door" I said.

The thoughts of that night were still fresh in my mind. That girl is a firecracker. I have to admit. Dottie had me hooked and I didn't want to go free. My thoughts were interrupted when Chris walked back into the studio and Patricia wasn't with him. I was going to ask him what is going on. He read it on my face. We have worked with each other for more than twelve years. He knew my faces.

"You wanted me to go get that bitch after that shit she did. I wanted to knock her mother fucking ass out. Fuck a lawsuit. I'll punch her ass to Afros" He said.

By now I couldn't stop laughing. That shit was funny. It's about ninety-seven degrees and he let her walk from the gate to the studio. He opened the door and let her in. She looked like she was in bad shaped. I kind of felt bad for her but I was through with helping her out. She wasn't going to play me.

I need to talk would be the first thing she would say. I prepared myself for it. I waited and waited but it never came. I was kind of surprised but didn't let her see it. She stood there dumb founded.

"I have a problem. I have been staying in a hotel for three months and now I don't have enough money to get home. All I'm asking for is a second chance or if you could help me get home. I promise I will never bug you again. I've been everywhere in Georgia to different labels but no one is interested, So sweet

Recordings, Off the chain Records, Criminology, and Bad Rap Records. No one even looked at me. I'm sorry I said those things about you. I was angry and frustrated. If you give me another chance I will not make you sorry please" She said.

Her speech touched my heart. Now could she be saying this because she has no place to go? She could be saying that because no other company will sign her. That she quit her job and got a big head (Oh … I got a record deal so fuck all of you, you can sick my dick). Now she wants me to let her ass back in no questions asked. She blew the advance money and now her supposed to be album is two months late. That's her fault.

Through all this I didn't realize that Dottie had come in and sat right next to me. She gave me a sweet kiss that knocked me back into reality. She had a bewildered look on her face and when I looked up I could understand why. Patricia was sitting on the floor on the top of the steps. The black plush carpet must be keeping her butt comfortable. She looked like a sheep dog about to be sold.

"I will tell you what. I will pay for your ticket and a taxi home and if I do let you come back you are going to have to pay for your own studio time. That is the only way this will work. If I see you are serious then I may match the money you put up. You have to show me that commitment. So I will help you get home but I will have to think about the other thing OK" I said.

She looked like the happiest donut in the shop. Dottie looked at me for an explanation. I put up one finger to signify (wait a minute).

"Patricia could you wait downstairs for a minute … I have to discuss something with Dottie.

"Chris … make sure that nobody comes in here" I said.

"You get it man" he replied as the door shut behind him.

"Why are you entertaining that thought? Do you remember what she said? I didn't hear what was said but I think you should rethink this one" She shouted!!!

"She told me that she spent all of her money on hotels and now she's stuck. She said she is sorry for behaving the way she did and for what she said. That she wants to make it right" I explained.

Dottie listened and twilled her fingers while I explained the conversation that she missed.

Now if I left her out it would be my fault because I brought her out here. Once she is at home she is no my responsibly unless I decide to help her again. Like I said if she puts up half of the money and shows the effort I will help her. Until I see it, she pays for studio time" I said.

"I see your point. I wouldn't want to be stuck out here either so if you go then I'm going with you (She said), I'll just let you know, that if she starts some shit … I'm going to knock her ass out".

"No problem" I replied.

Dottie and myself left the house around eleven o'clock. We reached the hotel Patricia was staying in. The hotel was on the edge of town closer to the airport than I thought. The entrance of the hotel was burned down a couple years ago. They never fixed that but the rooms were still in good shape. She was staying on the third floor. When we arrived at the room the door was open.

The room was small but nice. The beds on one side and the bathrooms adjacent to the kitchen. The brown carpet stood out considerately. Her bags were packed by the door. I instructed the butler to take the bags to the car. There was no sign of her in the room. That's when we heard noises coming from the bathroom.

"Uh … uh … uh … uh … uh … uh … uh oh my god … Fuck me"

I couldn't believe my ears she was fucking a guy in the bathroom. She had a plane to catch, and she's fucking a guy in the bathroom. I knew I should have left this bitch out to dry. Dottie gave me a look. I held my hand up to acknowledge what she was thinking. We had to take off at one anyway so we started to get into something of our own. I lay on the bed and she lay on top of me. We were kissing and rubbing all over each other when we suddenly realized where we were. She rolled beside me for a minute to compose herself when Patricia and her playmate entered the room. I never knew Patricia was gay. It really didn't matter given the circumstances.

I sat up in the bed and tried to collect my thoughts. All I had to do was get her on the plane and everything would be fine. Dottie looked at me funny look and I shook my head no. She lay back down, closed her eyes and shook her head.

All of a sudden without warning she got up and ran downstairs and got in the car.

"Patricia (I said) we have a plane to catch. We really have to go now" I said.

"I'll be right down" she said.

I went downstairs to where Dottie was, unlocked the car door, and got in. I understood the shock; but that was her personal preference. We had no decision making in this choice. It was all ready made, and decided. This was not our fault. I wanted to tell her this but I'm not sure she would hear me right now. She was still surprised by the fact that she was gay.

"Just let me do the talking ok" I asked?

"OK, but I really do get to knock her ass out right" she asked?

"Yes" I said.

"As long as we are clear on the fact" she said.

Patricia came to the porch and hugged her friend goodbye. As soon as she closed, the door we were on our way to the airport.

"I know you think that you can do this alone but, you can't. The only reason I am successful is because I have a few thousand people in my corner. They believe in some of the same things I do. Some where we find common ground and it works out" I explained.

She was listening attentively. I think she had a clue of what I was saying, but she was still angry. She sat there and folded her arms over her chest. If looks could kill Dot and I would probably be dead right now. We pulled up to the curb.

She watched as they put the bags on a trolley and began to wheel it directly to the plane.

Dottie and I moved swiftly through the airport. For one I didn't want to be stopped and two I wanted her out of my hair. I stopped at the watch stand and decided to purchase one. I only did it because I could. Dottie brought a pen and started to giggle. She handed me a piece of paper.

Patricia who was lagging behind run up to see what we were laughing at. I pulled the paper away before she could see it. She looked at me angrily; threw her hands up in the air.

"Fuck you" she screamed and walked away.

We hurried to the plane, the airports crowded and people started to look. Even though we passed her, she was still cursing.

"I don't know who the fuck they think I am. My name is Patricia and I demand respect. Fuck them. They don't know who I know. I got something for them". She said storming up the steps.

"I think it's going to be a long trip. The sooner this is over the better I will feel. I'm going to sleep so if you stay awake tell me when we get there" I replied.

"I would love to put her ass to sleep" Dottie said before the door closed.

I was going to be a long flight.

MEETING PATRICIA'S PARENTS

If the plane ride was a foretelling of meeting the parents I might as well leave now. All she did was whine and cry. Dottie slept most of the trip while I stayed in the cabin. For one she didn't agree with the relationship Dottie and I had engaged in. It really wasn't any of her business.

"I need to talk to you (she said with tears in her eyes) I see what you have with Dottie and I thought you wanted that with me. What … am I too young for you or is it that you despise me for some reason? I was willing to give you all of this (she showed off her figured from her feet to her head) and you told me no. I really think you are gay because anyone would want me (then she fell to the floor and began to cry) I just … wanted … to say … I … I … I … I love you. If only you could … you could love me back … the same way" She said.

Shit what could I say. I know it wouldn't work between us. She wanted too little I wanted too much. Besides the fact that she wasn't on the label anymore didn't change the fact that she might rejoin the fold someday, maybe soon. Plus in the last couple of weeks my relationship with Dottie had progressed into something that I would have never imagined it could be. She turned out to be better for me than Lisa ever had been. I mean Lisa was a wonderful girl but she let me get away with anything.

Dottie let me get away with a lot too but the bad things Lisa used to join me in, Dottie wanted no part of. So for me to be with her I had to quit the dumb shit. I think that's better for me anyway. That dumb shit almost got me killed and I still don't know why. I really need to find out.

"Have you been listening to me" she said (looking at me angrily)!!!

Her face was frowned up and she wanted me to get into a screaming match with her. That would make her feel really special.

"You're not … never mind" I said as I walked toward the rooms.

She just sat there and looked at me blankly. I wanted to say something encouraging but; there was nothing to say. The door shut behind me and that was the last time I even spoke to her.

The plane landed and she couldn't wait to get off. She got into the waiting car and didn't say a word. The wind howled as we rolled down the windows, the temperature was very low and even though we were cold the air was welcoming. Now Entering Wisconsin (the sign read a smile appeared on her face as the fields began to disappear and houses began to take shape).

"This wouldn't be a bad place to get way. I could buy a house here a couple of acres of land. You know really get some down time" I said.

"The Colorado Mountains is a better choice. Easier to get lost in" Patricia replied looking snidely.

"Yeah, but this area is more open. More airy don't you think" I replied giving her a don't fuck with me smile.

She sucked her teeth and began to stare out of the window again. It seemed like the temperature dropped ten degrees so we closed the windows. Dottie put her head on my shoulder and her hand in my lap. She told me countless times "I love being next to you". Patricia shifted her weight around so her head was blocking the view out of the right side.

"Right there" she screamed out!!!

We pulled up to a brown house that had a swing set in the front yard. She jumped out of the car, jumped over the gate and began knocking at the door feverishly. She waved both of us to come in. We looked at each other and shrugged our shoulders. I knew she wanted to say something but I started first.

"She is home safely. That was the plan. Now we can leave without any problems. This is over for me. For the time being I don't have any problems and I'm not going to start anymore" I said.

Patricia ran up to the car and stopped short of the window. I want you to meet my folks. Then she ran back up to the door. She knocked one more time and her parents answered. She embraced them as they did her. Like I used to hold my kids before they grew up. I still hold on to them sometimes too long, but they don't mind. She waved come on once again.

"I will go in for a little while but that's it ok" I said.

"OK" she said.

See Dottie loved things like this. Your family gets with my family and we meet each other. We got out of the car and walked past the grass to the door. It wasn't frozen over but the plants hid themselves underneath the ground. We made our way to the front door and embraced them as she did. They welcomed us into the house and we or I grudging accepted.

Green and Yellow covered the walls to match the green bay artifacts all around. If you don't think football fans take their team seriously here's proof they do. Patricia the mother (they call her Pat) walked into the living room with some tea. She offered us a seat, which we graciously accepted. Her Father (Mark) put on his Green Bay Jersey and sat down on the couch. Then he stood up headed for his favorite chair.

Patricia's brother came out of the room playfully and jumped in the chair. Mark punched him a few times playfully and he got up. He headed back toward the kitchen when Mark said "Phillip bring me a beer ... you don't mind if I drink do you MR ..."

"Smith (I responded) and no it's your home" I replied.

"We go by first names here" He said.

"OK (I said). My name is Devonte and this is Dottie".

"Dottie that's cute. So where are you all from anyway" He asked?

"I'm from Virginia and she is from Atlanta" I replied.

Mark called the whole family into the room. Patricia ran in and got everyone's attention. Her Dad, Mom, her Brother and her Friends, Phillips four friends had been in the back and came out when she did. Four women followed them. They had an awkward look on their faces. Now that she had everyone's attention she began to speak.

"This is Mr. Smith and Dottie, (she turned her attention to her family). This is my father Mark, my mom Pat, my brother Phil, Tracy, Shannon, Shellie, Lucy, Steve, Shawn, Lou, and Chris" she said introducing everyone.

Mark paused for a second. "Hey you're that rich guy that owns all the property and stuff. They call it Smith Inc. right. I knew you looked familiar your worth about six hundred million or something" He asked?

"About one" I replied.

"You gotta be worth more than that, he said.

"OK I'm a little under thirty billion right now" I replied.

"Show me a thousand. No ... No ... No ... five. Five thousand right now please" He asked?

I had fifty in my briefcase that was going to an orphanage after we dropped her off. I opened up the briefcase and they were all just dazed by how real it looked.

"Can we touch it' He asked?

"One at a time" I replied.

One at a time they came up and touched the money. They sat down and smelled their hands. I closed the briefcase putting it down by my side.

"That felt good (Phil said rubbing his hands on his face). So what is up with my sister's album? She can blow the windows off the room. When is it being released?

"Well (I said reading the expression on their faces which is not in my hands), all of that depends on if she does what she has to do. She has to jump on the situation that she has".

"What situation" Phil asked?

"Well (Patricia began to say) I wasn't doing anything in the studio and the advance money is gone. That's why they are here. They brought me home".

"How can we make this right" Her father asked?

"She has to pay for her studio time. Right now that's the only way she can get back into it. She has to get her focus back before we spend anymore money in this project" I replied.

He looked at her sternly "We sent you to California for your music career and you didn't do anything with it. That was a year ago where have you been, why haven't you called" He asked?

"We have enough money to get her started but not to finish" he said.

"If she shows she is committed to showing us and herself that she wants this than we will put up the rest of the money" I said calmly.

"We'll seeing as that you lost money already I would see why waiting is more beneficial to you. I also appreciate the offer" He replied reaching his hand out.

"Hold on(Phil said as he ran into the dining room, picked up several item from a box, dropped them back in the box and brought the whole thing. Then he eagerly set it down in front of me).

"This is our time capsule for school. They put me in charge of it this year. I was just thinking that if we could get ... I mean take a picture and put it in the time capsule we could put it in the ground tomorrow" He asked?

"That is not a bad Idea" I said.

Before we sat down to eat dinner we took a few pictures most of them that went into the box (time capsule) A few of them were hung around the house to remind them of my visit. It was a sweet gesture that I appreciated. They were having spaghetti with meatballs. As I ate I looked at the interior of the dining room.

It looked like they put a lot of money into that house. Hand made African ornaments hung on their walls while the chandelier had glass all around. The customized silverware was very unique. The knives had vines going down the middle with a sword at the end. At the end of the sword was the letter B. The table was set up nicely with flowerpot.

I was talking to Dottie about where we were going to stay tonight. Dottie wanted to stay at the Howard Johnson and I wanted to stay at the Sheraton Hotel. We finally made our choice and decided to leave. I had purchased round trip tickets in Atlanta by way of L.A. I placed the plane ticket on the table and stood up.

"Patricia if you want to do this, this is totally up to you. This plane ticket can be cashed in or used within the next three months. After that it is no good. If you do use it, call me when you get to L.A. and we can get everything started. Now that you see how hard it is you have to decide do you really what this. If you do don't blow it this time "I said.

I grabbed the briefcase from the front room and was walked to the front door. Mark and Pat greeted me there.

"It was really nice meeting you all" He said.

"It was a pleasure meeting you too" I replied.

It was only nine o'clock and it seemed colder that an iceberg. I opened the door and she climbed in quickly. I followed her and we were on our way in no time at all. She laid her head back and began to fall asleep. We arrived at the Holiday Inn and the cold air woke her out of her slumber.

We arrived at our room on the penthouse floor. She was already tired so I thought she would still be sleepy. Nope. She was full of energy. After I took my shower I waited for her. I lay up with my back against the pillows. Still she didn't come out.

I started to get worried but when I got out of bed, she came out. I was frozen in place as her silhouette sprang at me the light from the bathroom made her look like an angel. I didn't know where this ride was taking me but I did not want to get off.

As she walked over to me her robe dropped to the floor. I was aroused by what she was wearing. The bathroom light went out and the shadow of her began to more towards me. I reached out to grab her but she stopped. I put my hands down and she came closer until she was right in front of me.

"Now it's my turn" She whispered.

She took my shirt and began to rip it off of me. Then she tore my pants off leaving me with my drawls. She pulled of my drawls and saw that my dick was erect. She took it in her hand and started to rub softly. Then she took the strings that attached her top to her bottom and pulled them apart causing the top to fall to the floor.

"I need you baby" I whispered to her.

"Not yet" she replied smiling.

She began to take her thong off and by the time she finished, she began to suck my dick. As her tongue moved around my head she took her time to make sure she got every inch. Going deeper and deeper until she could take no more; she pulled it out and started to go faster until she felt what she wanted to feel. I was getting ready to cum. She pulled it out with enough time for her to absorb my cum.

"Shit girl" I said out of breath.

She didn't say anything she started to do it once again. She stood up still holding on to my dick. She wanted me to reach a point ... the point where I had taken her only nights earlier. This wasn't my thing. I loved to be in control, but this felt so good I felt like I was. She laid me down on the bed and began to move up my body.

Amazed my body was reacting to her and I could not help but show it. She had taken the stars away from the sky and now I was swimming and flying all at once. I closed my eyes and tasted her pussy. But I could also feel her sucking my dick. So I tasted it and dove in with lips, tongue, tonsils and everything I had. She kept giving it to me and I kept giving it to her.

This was a competition where there was no winner and there was no loser. She had taken me past that place to another. I closed my eyes and started to suck on her clitoris. She began to shake, rattle, and roll. She lost control of her body. She stopped holding on and just let go.

"AAAAAAAAHHHHHHHHHHH Shit make me cum ... Make me cum. I'm cumming. AAAAAAHHHHHHHHH SHIT" She screamed!!!

She still wanted more because her body was calling me and the phone was busy but I got through anyway. Just as quickly as I was making her cum she was about to make me ejaculate but she stopped. In turn I kept going taking her to the same place I was. She wanted to move but I kept her there. I wanted all that there was to get.

She was ready now. She turned around and wasted no time at all putting her pussy on top of my dick. She rode it in slow motion as my thrust met hers.

"AAAAAAAAHHHHHH" We screamed together!!!!!

We screamed for each other. We had all night to pleasure and fucked the shit out of each other but the night didn't have us and the cliff was coming up fast. She moved up and down, I moved round and round. She moved round and round I moved up and down. All that was left was air and she arched her back and I reached up and grabbed her. Then we released.

We stayed in that position for about a minute hovering over the sky over space, and then fell back down to earth. Now we were really one in the same. We shared the same space twice (not counting the outer times we've had sex). The same body, same mind, same spirit. There could have been a million people in this room and we were the only two that mattered.

BACK HOME

The next day was different. It was better we made a stop in California. I talked to some producers who might be interested in working with Patricia if she gets right. See in this business cash is king and I had plenty of it. I spoke to one producer named cure and he said that If the money's right we aight".

So we were only waiting on her. In the mean time they had other things. We had other things. Things ran smoothly all day. So when it was time to fly back to North Carolina I had no worries.

"Hey man what's going on" I asked?

"Hey everything is cool here man. You drop that girl off yet. Yo … I worked with a lot of people but she got an ego problem. Can't nobody work with that? Chris explained.

"I know man. I kept telling her that. I left her a ticket for L.A. Her parents said they would put up the money for her studio start". I said.

"If she does go who's paying for the rest of the sessions" He asked?

This is the part I Knew he wouldn't like. See Chris is a little high strung. Right is right and wrong is wrong. If I came right out and told him he would go crazy. So I had to break it to him lightly.

"Well if she shows that she really wants to do this and acts right … we are footing the bill" I replied.

"After all the stuff she put the company through in the first place. I hope you what you are doing. So where are you at right now" He asked?

'I'm on a plane flying to North Carolina. I'm gonna put down vocals for this album. There's nobody there so I won't have any distractions. So when I come back down there I will have it all together" I said.

"That's cool then I'll see you in" ... He started.

"Two months" I replied finishing his sentence.

"Bet that" He said. Then he hung up.

Before long the plane landed at the airport and slid to a halt. I agreed with Chris on a point. Once we put up the money we couldn't take it back. In all fairness it would take something extraordinary before we put the money up. We will see what happens with that.

Somehow, someway, the press was alerted of our arrival. There were about fifty or so reporters there so we could not avoid it. See Dottie didn't like reporters so I let her go out first. They sat by idly and waited for me to come out. I waited until she was safely in the car then exited the plane. I felt like I was at an art show. She rolled down the window smiled back to acknowledge.

David was in the crowd. I was surprised to see him here. I walked down the stairs and through the flashbulbs. I just couldn't shake the reporter.

"Mr. Smith ... Mr. Smith ... May we have a moment of your time please" She asked?

"Yeah sure" I replied.

"Word is that you're working on a new album. When is that being released, or is it finished" She asked?

"There still is a lot of work to be done, but It is halfway complete. As far as a release date I'm not trying to speak too soon. The album will be spectacular. I'm working very hard" I replied.

"So when can we get a peek" she asking grinning?

"You will be the first to know" I replied.

"Thank you" I replied as she gave me her business card.

I motioned for David to follow me into the limo. The door closed behind me. Dottie was curious to who he was. The powder blue shit and matching gators made an intimidating impression. The hat he wore made him look like a lonely cowboy. He took the hat off and old age appeared to be getting to him.

Dottie still had a precarious look on her face.

"Dottie this is David, David meet Dottie. Dottie is my lady. David is my father" I exclaimed!

Dottie eyes lit up with amazement. She looked like a chicken that was about to killed. She stuck her hand out almost upon reflex. She looked at him then looked back at me. It was taking awhile to get used to. That's the way it hit me I first found out.

"H … H … H … How are you doing. He never mentioned you" She said.

"He wasn't supposed to. My type of business requires that people think that I am dead. Now the only people that know I am alive are you and my son" David replied.

"What happen to what's his name" I asked?

"Do you mean my fake son? He tried to sell me down the river for the entire company. Snitch wanted all the control for his self. He didn't know that he wasn't my real son. I never even signed his birth certificate or anything. So I disappeared. They thought I was dead. Everything was transferred to you automatically. So I knew it would be safe to return and reclaim something" He said.

"That explained a lot. So what ever happened to him" I asked?

He was slow to answer as if he knows the answer would shock me. He looked down and pulled a bunch of paper out of his pocket. He reluctantly handed them to me. I had been focusing on one picture, the crime scene of my almost (accidental death) and my wife's murder.

"When everything went to you he found out that he wasn't my son. He had to leave the house, the cars, the money everything. He lost it. He ordered for your wife to be kidnapped. He wanted the money secondarily but he wanted to make you suffer. I was in the Bahamas and couldn't get back in time. When I did get back the deed was already done, except you killed his men. Unfortunately Lisa died and you spent six months recuperating. He doesn't know you are alive yet but by tomorrow he probably will. So he will be coming after you. My advice is to be careful" He said.

As he was talking I was figuring it out piece by piece. He would know for sure I was alive tomorrow. Knowing him even my name would attract his attention. So he would be coming after me. I'm ready for him. I'll give him everything he wants. Either he will find me or I'll find him.

We pulled up the long driveway to the house and my mind was now floating between hanging and cutting him up into little pieces. Dottie had started a conversation with David and was laughing about some childhood things I had done. My mind was on other things. The album was first. This album was important for everyone. In two months it would be complete, in three months on the shelves. After that I could take care of business. Everyday that went by though; it seemed it would become worse.

We entered the house to the sweet smell of potpourri. It looked as clean as the day I left it. I remember I could hardly walk, Dottie was just an illusion and my wife was still alive. Now it was different. It was a home me a Dottie could share. Lisa hadn't been here but once she said it was too country, too homey. If you ask me, she loved New York the most.

All these memories flooded me at once and I stopped at the stairs. I had to sit down for a minute. First, I wanted to cry then I wanted to scream. I think they both understood. They could only watch me as I suffered through my own private hell. The temptation had gotten to be too much I stood there flushed with madness. David and Dottie grabbed me sensing that I would do something destructive. I assured them that I was alright.

As soon as they let me go my anger flared up again and before anyone could stop me I had broke a vase that was on the table. I stared at that vase and started to say what I was thinking.

"That mothafucka is gonna pay for this shit. He took the person I cared about the most away from me. His ass is going down believe that" I said.

I looked back and saw everyone including house keeping staring at me. I walked to the patio and opened the door. I stepped out onto the balcony and soaked in the cool breeze. Dottie and David joined me on the patio.

What can I do right now. Nothing, I will settle this later. If I die I promise he will go ahead of me or we go at the same time. I haven't seen him for a year. He barked up the wrong tree. That's OK. When the time comes pay back will be dealt.

They were both looking at me like I was crazy. I just continued to soak up the air.

"So you came out of hiding to tell me this. How long did you know about this before you decided to come? What could you have done" I asked David?

"I only found out hours before the whole thing happened. Plus even though he thought I was dead if I told him to do or not to do anything he would listen. I still have the power over him…. Maybe more now. I called but by the time I got through, you were in the hospital. My people are still keeping track of him so if you need to know his whereabouts give me a call. I'll be at the house. (He gave me a hug and said) I love you. If you need my help call me.

He wasn't lying. I knew when he was bullshitting someone. He would take his time and answer slowly, making sure not to make a wrong statement or give the wrong information. He answered too quickly for this to be a lie. Plus he never offered to help me; he knew I wouldn't accept it. There must be something else to the puzzle. Something he couldn't tell me around Dottie. Later I will find out what it is but for now it was for work.

I took Dottie upstairs to the bedroom where I used to sit by the window. I shut the door behind me. There were flowers everywhere. Fresh flowers from the staff on card said.

We are sorry for your loss
And even though it must be hell
We know you will be able
To handle it very well
But even if you can't
Were always by your side
Cause you may sleep in many places
But here is were you reside (Home)

After I read it I gave it to Dottie. I was going to sit in that room all day but Dottie had a better Idea.

"Let's go for a swim" She said.

"Ok lets do it" I said.

She stripped down bear where she was. I wanted her right there. She was into her one piece in seconds. She bounced out of the room.

"Last one is a rotten egg" she hollered.

I was not going to lose this one. I changed into my suit and skipped steps all the way down. She was by the kitchen. I darted across the living room and took a short cut through the den. We both dived into the pool and hit the water at the same time. I came up to meet her eyes staring at me.

"You can't stand to lose can you" She asked?

"No. Can you" I asked?

"Not really but I'm beginning to love losing to you" she said.

"Well you're a nice complementary prize yourself" I said.

I swam to the edge of the water and jumped over the wall separating the Jacuzzi from the rest of the pool. I turned on the jets and the air bubbles began to rise. The temperature was nice and bearable. She moved closer to me and our sexual band began to tighten.

She moved underneath the water and began to suck my dick. She returned back underwater. It was unbelievable that she could hold her breath that long. Then she rose up and almost instantly put her pussy in my mouth.

I pulled the piece of her bikini to the side and begin to pig out. She almost slipped back into the water but gained composure enough to keep her shaking legs steady. She slowly leaned forward and put her breast in my face.

She slipped back into the water and inserted herself onto me. She moaned upon the sensation of her moving up and down on top of me. This was her moment. She wanted it. I couldn't take that away form her. It was beautiful.

I could tell she was feeling it. She arched her back and began to rock back and forth. The vibration plus her movement was making me lose control. We fell into the water and breathed a sign of relief.

I think we both needed that. The Patricia situation and now this? She was chilling lying with her head back without a care in the world. I on the other hand do. I have several meetings next month (good thing there all in the area because I will be busy getting this album ready).

We frolicked in and around the pool all day. I knew that this is just what I needed to get my mind off things. I got out of the pool and fired up the grill around six. It never fails that neighbor's drive over whenever they smelled Barbeque, and since I like to cook a lot of food. I opened the gate and they flooded in.

I love this neighborhood. Some people brought chips. Some brought hot dogs. A whole lot of people brought the sodas. The homeboys down the street brought the music and the DJ. So it turned into a party within minutes. Several people came up to me during the party to share their condolence about Lisa. I introduced them to Dottie and they took to her nicely.

She was out there singing and dancing having a ball but every once in awhile. She would look over at me to make sure I was alright. A couple of clowns busted in and tried to brush up on her but once the neighbors knew she was with me, they weren't letting that happen.

We bounced them clowns up out of there and continued to party. I knew whatever happened I could come here and everything would be fine.

FAMILY BUSINESS

I have been locked up in my studio for about a week putting down vocals. I only came up for air to shower and sleep. My meetings haven't started yet so I'm slaving over this board. I feel re-energized and I love it. I let Dot come down and hear some of it. A couple of tracks needed a woman voice so I gave her a microphone, some instruction and some magic happened.

I think without pushing it this album could be done in two months. Still, there's no word about Patricia. She didn't go to California or she hasn't called me. Once I lay down my vocals anyone who wants to get on can do so. There are about twenty tracks so there is plenty of room.

My phone is ringing constantly off the hook. The album is hot and it's not finished. I know Lisa would be proud of me, and even though I miss what we had Dottie and I have a beautiful thing going on now. The music is thumping and my brain is ratting with ideas. The beats are hypnotic and I am more hypnotized by Dottie's voice. It's like a bird singing.

D and Ray have been here for the last few days. They said (We need a break from our wives. So their wives came along too. They just wanted to get out of Atlanta. I don't blame them really. That's why they go on some tours with me. They get to see some other countries but don't have to stay if they don't want to plus they kept me company on my down time. The girls are spending time with Dottie.

My house is tucked behind three-miles of trees in a private area. It's not huge but it kind of resembles the Whitehouse but with more land. Indoors and outdoors pool, studio beside the game area. The theater is on the second floor next to the pool (Billiard) room that has seven tables. My garage is downstairs and has seven cars parked in it. I also have a personal basketball court on the premises (Smith's House). Last but not least I have a helipad to take me right to my plane.

That is how everyone else got here. Francine is Ray's wife. She's five-seven, very curvy and cute. They have been together for six years now and got married. The reception was beautiful and they now have a son together named Brian. Brian is about six months old and smart. He likes books and smiles a lot.

Stephanie is kind of different. D said he would never fall in love but when he met her he couldn't help. We were at a party and he spent the whole night with her. They have been married for three years and going strong. I have never seen him so happy before.

D and Ray were in the studio with me while Stephanie, Dottie and Francine were in the pool. Every now and then they would come down and see what was going on. They made us take breaks (which were necessary) because we would be in there for weeks at a time. By the end of the month fifteen tracks were done. There were people who wanted to be on the album but I had to be selective. This was more than an album this was a musical photo album.

As time would have it a month and a half has passed; and the album is almost completed. A few people who I have called came through and put down some verses but other than that, that's it. Curiosity, Menace, Nympo, and a few members of black dragon family showed up but no more. The end result came out the way I wanted.

I packed up the masters and grabbed the CD of the finished product. I ran up to the house and went into the theater. I ran my hand across the suede that covered the floor and walls. I was feeling for a little latch (that would open the safe). I found it and a section popped out of the wall revealing the safe. I punched in the code and the door swung open. I opened the bottom compartment and put the CD in with the money.

I kept plenty of money around so just in case I get into an emergency I can have it. Once I closed it back I closed the safe door and wall panel. I flicked the switch on the wall to seal the panel. I made my way to the meeting room. I had a series of meetings to observe. After they say what they have to I made a decision.

The top discussion was record deals and contracts, who's out, who's in, who's new, who's fresh, and who's hot. I took my seat at the head of the table and opened my folder. I took a look up from the folder to focus on the chandelier hanging from the ceiling. It seemed so much clearer for some reason. Anyway I shrugged it off and kept looking around the room. Everyone had not arrived yet so there was a little time to kill.

The walls of the room were black as well was the carpet. I had it that way so my platinum plaques came out more. Besides from the gold material on the chairs and the platinum table there wasn't much left in the room. I had my laptop so that even while I was in the studio I could still see what was going on.

My daughters Lakisha, Andria and my son Deion came in and sat down. About five years ago I found out I had three children by a women in my past relationship. It came as a shock because I had just found Lisa and straightened out my (problems). I had a lot of bad Karma coming at me because of what I had done. I have straightened most of it out but something just keeps popping up. Now it's the Vinni situation.

I love my children very much. They now do internships at several of my businesses during the summer. Since they are staying with me during school I stopped touring so I could be with them. They smiled and opened their folders. The meeting was ready to begin.

Chris used to be one of my top artists, but he now has his own label. He also took over when I wasn't there. Since I started to concentrate on the business end, it let him become more creative. I think he respects me more for what I gave up than for what I have. It was hard to give up touring and everything. I have to do what is best for my people.

If I were out on tour and something happened at the office only I could handle (which has happened before) I have to probably cancel the show. Chris AKA (crazy legs) was my first artist. He picked up where I left off. He carried a lot of weight on his shoulders and I have a lot of respect for that. We carried each other along with D, Bo, Art, Shawn and Richie Rich (now deceased).

Chris started off the meeting.

"This meeting is in session. The topic for this week's meeting is the direction we are going as a company. We have made great strides but I think we can to even further. We have to improve on the little things and to make sure everyone is on the same page. With that said I turn meeting over to Mr. Smith".

"Thank You Chris (I said). We are hitting high numbers in our marketing, trading, entertainment, and small business areas. The economy is growing and we have a large part to do with that. With that said I have reviewed the paperwork on some contracts and signed off already.

I passed a copy of the signed contracts around.

"These are mostly people who have to renew this year. Mr. Warner replied. (He represented the parent company we took over). You are just going to keep things the way they are" He asked?

"Yes and No" I replied.

"Explain this to me" he said forcefully.

"By resigning the current artist and signing new artists, we keep fresh money flowing. Plus people want things of their own. You know business and what not. I am not trying to hold people back like you all used to" I said.

"What do you mean like we used to" he asked angrily?

"When I first signed, I signed for four years. During that time I made you a ton of money and you were happy. When I wanted to renew my contract I asked for my own imprint. You didn't want to give it to me. Not until I almost signed with someone else, you gave me a new a contract. It just so happens, even though I was making you all that money you ran out. By then I had enough money to buy you out so I did and now you work for me. So now even if I do make a bad decision you are not going anywhere because no one else will pay you enough to keep the house or the ride you got right" I asked?

He looked down at the folder like he was looking for something. He just got cursed out in the nicest way possible. There were a few chuckles and some looks that made me want to laugh. Business had to go on though. So I moved on to the three artists we were probably going to sign. I read their profiles out loud.

Karen Baker (Sphere). She chooses the name because she feels she is better rounded than most female's rappers in the game. She is five foot nine, one hundred fifty pounds. She has green eyes and a bangin body. I would go after her myself. She hails from Memphis but lives in New Orleans. I like her because she has something she wants to prove and she had the skills to do it.

Marcus Bell (Cyclone). He has done many talent shows and won must of them. He has sent tapes of his performances and I have to admit he is very impressive. He is a big dude but he carries his weight well. He hails from Philly and has shopped his demo to only one company, mine. He said that this is the only record company I want to work with because I want to get the best opportunity I can. He's six feet, two inches. He could be very intimidation but that doesn't faze me. His flow is sick and I can't let him get away from me.

Nathan K Hobbs AKA Hooks. He calls himself the ultimate hook. He needs a little help to find his style but his potential for extraordinary things is impressive. His frame is not that big one hundred eighty five, five foot eight but his confidence is so much bigger. I met him a few months before the accident and he came back stage to talk to me. He comes from North Carolina. His thing is singing. He hits his notes solidly and has a wide vocal range. There is no limit (with work) to the things he can do.

I wrote my comments down and passed them around the table for a final vote. The fact that I like all the artists should make it easier for their decisions. Still there are a few that I am not sure of.

Out of the eight people sitting at the table beside me the ones I was worried about a little were Mr. Green, Mr. Harper, Mr. Warner, Mr. Styles, and Mr. Steel. I had just talked to Mr. Warner so he wouldn't be a problem. Even though I can approve anyone I want, the artists still have to work around these people. The last thing I need is tension where there is none.

"So write down your decisions on a piece of piece of paper and pass them up. I need honest answers. We can talk about why's later" I said.

After the votes were counted and the announcement was made I had the pleasure of calling each of them and telling them they were signed to the label. I was about to get up and leave when Mr. Harper stood up.

"What about Patricia Dobbs" Mr. Steel asked?

Shit. The one subject I wanted to avoid. All the other meetings were about budget and the little shit. This … this was huge. They don't know what happened at the house. They don't know I kicked her out. They don't know I got shot. They don't know shit right? Well my decision was simplified by the fact I gave her a plane ticket that is good for a month and a half. That would be the last of it. I would tell them that. Then there would be no more questions about it.

I started to tell them but as I glanced over to Chris. His face was covered in pain like someone hit him. My face would look like that but I had to answer the question. Apparently me children had heard because they were shaking their heads no. They don't know about the conversation I had with her parents so it was OK … Maybe.

"Well (I said hesitating). There is a problem with that … but it's beyond my control" I said.

Mr. Styles asked "What do you mean"?

"She went back home. She said she needed to around her family to decide what she wanted to do. (I looked back around the room and the painful expressions seemed to disappear slightly). I took her back to Wisconsin and had a talk with her parents. I told Patricia to come to California when she was ready to do some work. I left a plane ticket so she could come back. Her parents will pay for the first part of the studio time and if progress is made we will cover the rest" I replied.

"Why did you do that for? Tell her we will cover all her studio time" Mr. Styles yelled!!!

My face started to turn when I realized an easy solution.

"OK I'll call her right now" I replied.

I dialed Patricia's house and she answered the phone.

"Hello" she said.

"Hello how is you" I replied?

"I'm OK. I really want to do this and I know I messed up but I'm ready now. The only thing is that … My Parents can't come up with the money" she said sounding up set.

"Well I got the guys here and they are willing to help with the studio time" I replied.

"Oh … really? WOW. I will be in LA next week. I give you a call next week when I get there thank you guys" she said.

She hung up the phone.

"I want to thank you for helping me out of a very tough situation. You have just volunteered your services to pay for her studio time" I replied.

All at once Mr. Green, Mr. Harper, Mr. Styles. And Mr. Steel stood up in protest.

"Well, I replied, if you want her on the label then you will pay for it. If you don't want to pay for it than you tell her that she doesn't have a contract. She informed me that she would be in California in one week so decide what you are going to do. If you want to quit I will accept you resignation" I said sternly.

There was a long pause as smiles appeared almost all the way around the room.

"Exactly what would we be billed for" Mr. Styles asked?

"Vocals, technical things, shows, appearance, practices, range lessons plus a few other things" I said.

"So am I to assume that you are resigning or are going to crush someone's dreams and tell then they don't have a contract" I asked?

"There are plenty of record labels that would want a director like me. You will have my resignation by five" Mr. Styles yelled.

"Me too" replied Mr. Harper, Mr. Steel and Mr. Green.

"I will need that in writing but once you leave this room you've already quit" I said.

Mr. Styles, Mr. Green, and Mr. Steel left the office and were out of the drive-way in no time. Mr. Harper sat back down. I knew him too well. He was not going to leave and not have something lined up elsewhere.

"So, he said, what happens now" he asked?

"We get little missy into the recording studio. Oh don't worry your friends will foot most of the bill. See they are signed for four more months. If they resign they are in breach of contract. If they are insubordinate I can fire them and they don't collect a dime. So either way they paid for her. Even if she does work or not I don't have to worry about a thing" I said.

He had his face down in his hands. I couldn't help but feel sorry for the guy.

"You don't have to pay anything (I told him). I'm going to send you down to the mailroom for a while. They need some help down there. In the meantime, that warrants a cut in pay and I will need your keys now".

He hung his low and handed me the keys to the car he drove. I would make sure he got home. I had to get cars back from those other three guys so figured if I reported them stolen I would get then back quicker.

After everyone had left (I mean Mr. Harper) I called everyone into the theater and showed them the finished product. It was time to start promoting and everyone was eager to get started. I had the right people in my corner to pull this off so the ball started to roll full speed ahead.

FRESH BEGINING

It's six o'clock. Patricia's plane just landed. The temperature at LAX is ninety-four and my bottle of water is almost gone. She called from the plane and said she would be on the ground shortly. So when she came around the corner, bags in tow I was relieved. Hopefully she would fulfill her commitment and record this album, but the fact that she was here showed where her commitment was.

As she approached me she smiled. She dropped her bags and whispered the words thank you in my ear. I smiled at her and ushered her into the car.

"So where do you want to go first" I asked?

"I am kind of hungry. I haven't eaten breakfast yet", she replied.

"OK. Charlie stops at the breakfast spot. I am kind of hungry myself" I said.

It was a half an hour ride when we pulled into the restaurant. I got out and waited for security to flank me. Patricia joined me and we followed the information one in the front, one in back, and one on each side. We entered the restaurant and were led immediately to our table. We sat at a table close to the window so I could see who was coming and going. Patricia sat with her back facing the door.

What would you like for breakfast" The waitress asked?

"Well I will have the waffles, bacon, scrambled eggs with cheese and a glass of orange juice with a side of hash browns, could you also bring a couple cups of coffee over please" I asked?

"I will have the same along with some toast" Patricia replied.

The waitress took down the order and headed toward the kitchen. I could tell she recognized me but didn't want to make a scene. She started to get excited as she told her co-workers. The excitement spread to the kitchen. After awhile the waitress came along with the drinks. She leaned over close to me and whispered.

"My co-workers want to say hello" She said.

"No problem. Send them over" I replied smiling.

So one by one they came over and I signed their piece of paper. They were so excited. It made me remember how it feels to not be who I am. The food seemed to be taking forever. I wonder was I the reason the food was taking so long because even the cook came out for my autograph. I was about to call the waitress over when a tray of food was headed our way. The waitress unloaded our food and whispered, "thank you". She kissed me on the cheek and ran off.

I picked up my knife and folk and began to eat. The eggs were done perfectly and the bacon was nice and crisp. The waffles were light and fluffy and the hash browns (which I don't usually eat) were to die for. The restaurant itself was nicely decorated.

There were about fifty or sixty tables. About twenty booths outlined the rest of the restaurant. There were ceiling fans all over the place and fifteen seats at the bar area. The jukebox in the corner was playing some oldies. The rough worn orange and red rug created an appropriate eating habit. I called the waitress over and order a second helping.

"So how does it feel" Patricia asked?

"How does what feel" I asked?

"You know, being famous everybody knowing your name. I mean your album is going to be in stores and everyone knows your face. I bet it feels good. I was thinking about that earlier and it scared me. That's why I stopped going to the studio. I didn't want to put out an album then not be able to go anywhere without cameras following me. I talked to my parents and now I understand that is a part of fame. I think I can handle it now" She said.

"If you needed someone to talk to all you had to do was call me. I would have helped you out. I need to clear my head sometimes too. Knowing you have someone to talk to makes difficult situations seem easier. So for now on if you have any questions all you have to do is ask me" I replied.

"Cool" she replied.

While I finished off the second helping of food the waitress just delivered she stood up and went to the bathroom. The second round was more delicious then the first plate I ate. I leaned back in the chair to give my stomach room the breath. She came back and sat down. I stood up and grabbed my jacket. I took out two hundred dollars and dropped it on top of the bill. She stood up and followed my lead as I headed toward the door. With security behind Patricia and me we piled into the car, while they got into the other car.

"So are you ready to hit the studio yet or do you wanna get settled first" I asked her?

"I'll just drop my stuff off first" she replied.

"Okay" I replied.

"We are very close to the studio so that won't be a problem" I said.

I pulled up into the parking lot and the Black Benz came to a stop. The valet came over to get the car but I brushed him off. I called the baggage handler over. I gave him a fifty and asked him to take the bags up to my room. As he disappeared into the hotel my foot hit the petal and the wheels began to take the same motion that the rims were spinning. My bodyguards were trying to keep up as I weaved through traffic.

Fifteen minutes later we pulled into Black out studio. It was located in a well-populated area. The parking lot was full. I pulled into the spot reserved for me. Two minutes later the black escalade truck pulled into the spot beside me. They hopped out looking upset but couldn't stop laughing. I killed the engine and exited the car. Patricia came around the front of the car and we all entered the studio.

"You really need to stop that. You're gonna crash that thing on day" Brad said.

"That will never happen. I'm too good for that" I responded.

The entrance was well lite. There were offices on either side of the black-carpeted hallway. The beige walls made the dragons on the carpet come to life. The first four offices were meeting rooms. The offices in the back were for different labels (six to be exact). We made our way to the studio in the back. As I reached the door the Dottie appeared and wrapped her hands around me. Patricia stopped behind me.

"I missed you" she whispered after she laid a sweet kiss on my cheek.

"It's only been two hours. Here I brought you some breakfast. I got it just like you like it. Buttered toast, scrambled eggs with cheese, grits, and sausage" I replied smiling.

"Thanks" she said she skipped into the back room.

All the tension and hostility seemed to disappear as they embrace her and them the same. There was a new attitude as everyone including Patricia seemed to concentrate on work. I walked in and took a seat at the board. This one is different so I have to familiarize myself with it. After everyone is seated and the door is closed, I got everyone's attention.

"Well my album comes out in a week and there will be a lot of things going on. I know a lot of you that have albums coming out put the main priority is this album right here. We are already three months behind and the other board members what to see something. We have a month to give them a sample. So anyone with any ideas ... don't be afraid to speak up ok" I stated.

There was nothing but silence as I turned back around to face the board. I turned it on and the room came to life with sound. I missed that feeling. The feeling you get when you are creating something the world will hear. To share your experiences with other people, to see your own creativity come true ... to help someone out of a jam. That is the type of music I love to make.

I started messing around with certain tracks breaking them up and down until I got the right feel for one. Patricia come up and sat beside me. I am glad to see her so enthusiastic about a project that only a month and a half ago she didn't want anything to do with.

It took us all day but by the end of it, we had something to start with. It was about six o'clock and I was really tired. Patricia was very enthusiastic and didn't want to stop so we finished and started another one. I could tell that for the time being she really wanted the fame and the stardom. She had the drive to obtain it. All she had to do is keep it up.

We (me and Dottie) created a real rapport with each other. Patricia was getting closer to us and even apologized for the thing at the house. I forgave her for two reasons. One if I didn't she would be hurt and in order to work with her I had to throw it away.

She started putting down vocals for the first record and I was truly amazed by her voice quality. Dottie and her would have singing contest to see who would win. They were both really good. I had the brilliant idea of putting them on a record together. After that one week we had completed two records.

By this time other producers started to come in and work with Patricia. This meant I could spend some time at the Penthouse with Dottie. I drug myself out of the studio and handed my keys to cliff. I climbed into the passenger side and sat back. I ... we (me and Patricia) have been up for four days straight. Before I could pull off she was being carried out of the studio.

"Ya'll go home, get some rest and be back up here in two days ... I am going to get some sleep" I said.

"Alright see ya in two" Chris said.

The car pulled off and we were headed for the hotel. I must have fallen asleep because I opened my eyes and we were at the hotel.

"Patricia ... Patricia ... come on and get up. We gotta go" I whispered.

"Do … dodo … dodo … dodo … dodo … dodo … dodo …" she replied.

I grabbed her hand and she raised, half sleep, out of the car. We made our way to the lobby. After Brad parked the car he escorted us to the elevator. Forty floors up and we were on the floor. I don't even remember the lobby. There just a lot of bright lights and chandeliers. The furniture looked comfortable. Anything would look comfortable after five days of work. We slept for a little but it wasn't enough. Dottie kept telling me (You're gonna burn yourself out).

The minute I hit the bed I was out like a light. Dottie began to pull my clothes off and started to run the shower. Thirty minutes was enough so I thought. Nope I was wrong. After I finished I still felt like I needed a bath. The water was already made so I got in. I felt invigorated and when she got it, she started to play with me thinking I wouldn't respond.

Wrong again, I pulled her on top of me. I held her closely to me and kissed her softly. I parted her lips with my tongue. She melted like butter. She had been waiting for me and she let me know as her tongue roamed around my mouth.

As her mouth was locked to mine catching any breathe of air that tried to escape. Her body felt good against mine. She adjusted herself on top of me. She put her hands on the edge of the tub while I adjusted my hands on her hips, helping her move up and down.

It didn't matter how tired I was, I wanted this. She could tell and began to pump harder as I went deeper. This crazy web we had spun had reached new heights when she began to shake uncontrollably. Trying unsuccessfully she willed her body to my bidding. The faster I moved the more she lost control. Her back arched and she began to reach for the sky.

"Shit … Fuck me … damn it … AAAHHHHHH Shit … Fuck … fuck … fuck … do that shit" she screamed!!!

I found myself losing control so just like she allowed I willed my body to her. Slower and faster she moved I was ready to blow. I laid my head back and closed my eyes. The pressure was building as I held on for a long as I could.

"AAAAAAAAHHHHHHHHHH …" I screamed!!!

"AAAAAAAAHHHHHHHHHH shit …" she screamed!!!

After we lay there for a minute I finally began to pull myself out of the tub and dry off. I pulled on my robe and made my way to the dresser. I pulled on my underclothes and crawled into bed. She followed behind me. She liked to sleep naked so she took off the robe and towel, then crawl under the covers. I could feel her warm body next to me as we drifted off to sleep.

Sixteen hours later I was awakened by a huge hamburger with fries. It's a little off my usual food choice but I was starving. I went into the front room and took a seat at the table. Patricia had just got out of the shower and had already got dressed. She looked refreshed and ready to go back to work. She was tearing into the food just like I was doing. After four burgers, and fries and coca cola I had reached my quota of food.

Monday I had to hit the stores and promote this album. I knew it was going to sell but I also had to lead by example. My first signing was downtown in the Ritz, than Sam Goody. So I only had a little bit of time to enjoy myself. I sat down and turned on the TV. Every other commercial on bet was advertising the release of my album. If Vinni really wanted to find me, he would know right where to look.

"Patricia, I left about twelve tracks at the studio if you want to use them. Chris knows what he is doing so u can trust him. I will be gone for about two months, but I want you to work like you would if I were here. Do one thing for me though. Make sure you get a lot of rest ok. Don't let the work rule you. You rule the work. These are the hottest producers so be sure what you want. If you have any questions about anything you can ask Chris or call me. By the time I get back your album should be over half done" I said.

"Okay. See you in two months" she replied.

"You can stay here while your recording, I already set it up" I said.

She smiled as Dottie and I headed to the other apartment. I turned the key and the Benz roared to life. I pushed the pedal and we were off.

Jump'in Off

Now with Patricia back in the studio, that gave me one less headache. It wouldn't be long before Vinni came after me. I know how he would do it to. He would come after me alone. No family, no friends, just me. I have another month in the studio than I have to go on tour. The problem was not that big, yet.

Patricia was doing great. The label had kicked in their half of the money and I added mine. She was finished most of the album and has become a real fan of Dottie. On her off time they would lay in the back by the pool. Patricia had a nice figure and the other guys noticed. I had to issue them a warning. I walked into the pool area and Patricia was talking to Ron. I walked over to the table and sat down.

I waved Chris over and told him to tell everyone to come to the table. I think they knew what I was going to say because a few people started to frown.

"I think you all know what I'm going to say. This project is very important to the label and I see something happening. Yes. She is very pretty and I know you all have noticed. I know you all know of Patricia's track record so far. This time it's pretty good, last time was very poor. I want things to stay the way they are or to improve. I need you guys to cool it out when it comes to her. I need her focused the way she is now in order for her to finish. All of ya'll know what it's like. Just getting in the game ... fresh start ... new label whatever your situation, I want her to keep what she had and romance is her weakness. After the album is done maybe but you follow company policy anyway. You don't mess with other artists on the same label. Just remember I hear everything so don't sneak anything past me or try to because you will be gone" I said.

I rose up from the table and left them there. Patricia was in the kitchen getting some iced tea for herself and Dottie. She grabbed two glasses and put them on the tray. She grabbed the pitcher and poured two glasses or tea. Gently setting the pitcher on the tray, she scooped some ice and put some in each glass. She grabbed the ice bucket and put that on the tray. She took the tray and made her way to the pool area where she set it on the table. She came back in and sat next to me. Glass of tea in hand, she took a sip than placed it back on the table.

All the while I was reading my newspaper. I saw that she was eyeing me awkwardly, and then she dropped her eyes to her glass.

"What's up" I asked as I put down newspaper?

"I just wanted to say thank you again for a second chance. Most people would have probably let me go without a second thought" she said.

"Well, I replied, I have always said you are very talented. So I was more than wiling to give you a second chance. Everyone needs to be heard (she smiled and dropped her head; flattered), even you. Now on this last part you have to really be focused. The executives have liked what they heard so far so the last eight don't have to be super-duper. I just want you to do the best U can do. I have to leave in a month so I am going to push you hard.

"Ok. If I finish this album can I go on tour with you" she asked?

"Let me think about it Ok" I replied.

That wasn't a bad idea. She could be finished with the album it's three weeks barring any setbacks. Plus someone needed to be replaced and she needed the exposure. No sooner than I could pick my paper back up John came running and sat down.

John was my head caretaker. He did an excellent job. He was also the coolest one on staff so something must really have him shaken. I put down my paper.

"What's wrong" I asked concerned?

"Mr. Vinni is here to see you" he said.

"Where" I asked?

"Down the street, by the gate" He said.

My head was zooming. I saw Patricia and the guys headed to the studio. I ran to the box where I kept the keys to all the cars. I took the keys to the BMW and ran out the front room. I was already out the front door when they reached it. I jumped in my car and without a word the engine roared to life and I took off down the driveway. While I waited for the gate to open I saw the black navigator pull up and I pulled the car over. I thought to myself (I better go with someone). I got out and jumped in the truck.

"Drive to the end of the block" I said.

It didn't take that long to get there doing twenty-five for a minute or so. The street was long. In order to get in view of my house you have to get past five blocks and another street. I say it's (the block). We arrived at the gate and the scene was like dejavu. Just like before.

Last time they came up to the gate at my house so I moved back further. I got out of the car and my boys D, Bo, and Ray, followed behind. I left all of my bodyguards behind. I gave the security guard twenty dollars to get some lunch, in other words ignore what was about to happen.

I walked up to the gate and turned around to hear the screeching tires. My security jumped out of the van and began to approach but I told them to stay back. I turned back and saw Vinni telling his people the same thing.

He approached the gate by himself. He got a lot of balls. To bad he was going to loss them.

"What do you want" asked already knowing?

"How long have you known I wasn't his son" he asked?

This was personal. I told the boys to step back and not interfere. They didn't understand that I didn't want anyone involved. Reluctantly they did what I asked only because I would do it for them.

"I knew from that day he called me to the house. He said you would be pissed when you found out. I wanted to laugh but some reason I just couldn't. He knew that you would come but not when. I can't do this now so if we can get together later that would be cool" I said jokingly.

"So you got everything and I got nothing. Is that how it's supposed to go" H asked?

Things were getting really serious. I looked back and called my boys up. Before he could call his, I jumped over the pole and punched him dead in his jaw. My boys came over and pulled out their guns. That stopped his people in their tracks. I continued to hit him until he hit the ground and didn't get up.

"If you have a problem with that … come find me and we will settle this again" I said as I was walking away.

I hopped back over the pole and got in the car. D, Ray and Bo followed. My security got in the other vehicle and we all watched the bodyguards pick his body up and carry him to the car. They took off and I could tell that they weren't happy. D looked at me and laughed.

"You didn't have to hit that hard. I think you broke his jaw" he said.

"I did" I replied.

I know I broke something. I broke his jaw, a couple of ribs and the way he landed I'm pretty sure his arm or leg if not both are broken. I had to do it like that. Three months I'll be touring the US and he will still be recuperation. I had to buy some time.

We pulled back into the gate and I jumped out. I got in the Benz and drove up to the house, followed by my bodyguards and D, Bo, and Ray. Dottie was waiting at the door when I pulled up. I killed the engine and jumped out of the car. I walked up the steps and looked at her. She was looking at my bloody and bruised hands.

She grabbed me as I began to walk by her.

"What happened to your hand" she asked?

"Vinni" I replied as I walked toward the kitchen.

Dottie followed behind me and got some Ice and rag. She cleaned up my bloody fist with a wet rag and wrapped my hands in some ice with a towel. She sat down next to me.

"Now who is Vinni and why are you bleeding" Dottie asked?

It took me all of forty-five minutes to tell her about David which she already met who is now kicking back in the backwoods. I also told her about how Vinni was out and now wanted revenge. I told her what happened at the gate and she seemed to get a little scared.

"What if they come after me or your children" she asked?

"They will not come after you or the children. He will come after ME ... No one else. That's why I hit him. If I had shot them, they would come after all of us. I only got him. He is going to tell them he wants revenge and come after me. He's not dumb or stupid. If he sends someone I will know and he's not ready to die yet so he won't go after people I love. Also he does not want the rest of the people he loves dead, that I haven't killed. It's just going to be him and me. Since he is going to have to recover that will be about three to six months before he does anything. So don't worry OK" I said.

"You seem like you know what you are talking about" she replied.

"No I know him" I said.

The incident was pressing on my mind so I got back in the studio with Patricia. Anytime I get into music I forgot about problems momentarily. Plus Patricia is so talented she could make a bluebird cry. So that's what I did. I buried myself in work. Other producers came through and added their sound to the album and I have to admit the album came out sounding tight.

We had two weeks left before the deadline but were finished the album. Patricia said she wanted to add a more personal touch to the album. So we ended up having twenty-one songs on the album. Personally the last three songs made me cry and Dottie needed to leave after the second song just to be able to hear the third.

Now Patricia is starting to believe she can do it. That's what was missing the drive, the want, and the need. Now that she had the hunger she felt like she was ready.

After we finished mixing the album and sent it off to press, she came upstairs in my office while I was in a meeting with the executives the door was open so she just walked in. She took the seat next to Dottie and waited for everyone to stop talking.

She raised her hand like she was in school. I already knew what she wanted. I needed to know how serious she was about it. Tours can be a terrifying thing.

"Yes" I said.

"I'm going on tour with you whether you like it or not" she said sternly.

"Ok. No problem. We leave in a week" I replied.

She jumped across the table and into my lap saying (thank you, thank you). Then she ran out of the room to go tell the others. She had a right to be excited. She earned it.

Roll'in Around

We just finished a show in Chicago last night and now we've landed in Detroit for our show tomorrow. After three shows in four days, everyone was tired. Dottie came up to see me and we spent the day together. It's been three weeks and even she is tired but she is still having fun. Last night the crowd was on fire. Half the time they cheered her name (Patricia, Patricia) or mine.

In fact, they gave her a nickname (Patti). As soon as she came out on stage the crowd started to chant Patti, Patti, Patti, Patti, Patti. Even her mother and father came out to give her support. She loved that the most. The album wasn't even out yet so I know once it hit the shelves it would sell like hot fire.

I was having a meeting over the phone when the thought occurred to put the album out sooner. It was supposed to come out in October, why not put it out in September. The execs would think that was a good idea. I would call them and make that happen. So I called once I hit the hotel.

"Rick" I shouted in the receiver!!

"Yeah, I can hear you fine man. What's going on" He asked?

"Fifty to seventy thousand a show ... Man you tell me" I said.

"I saw your girl on TV. She's doin her thang got dem boys goin crazy right" He said.

"Yeah (I said). Look ... do me a favor ... I want you to move the release date up on the album. The way the tour is going. We will have to print triple just to keep on the shelves. They are lovin her right now" I replied.

"Not a problem. Consider that done. I'll move it up two weeks. Do you know what's going on with Shawn's (timetable)? He's talking about payin more attention to Patricia than you are anyone else. Everyone else is cool with it but he's talking bout leavin the label. What should I do" Rick asked?

"Tell him to call me. I will explain everything to him. Let me talk to him and calm him down OK" I replied.

"OK man. Later" he said.

I'm not going to let this bother me right now. The tour is a hit and people from Louisiana are coming up north to catch it. Everyone knows what's going on. I'm doing what's necessary. I'm her hype man and she's my hype girl. I'm going to call him and find out what's going on.

The show was at five o' clock so I would be on the plane to St. Louis by eleven o' clock. I was tired afterwards but at the same time I was amped the rush, the thrill, all of the fans screaming. I thought about all of that so I was kind of blown when Shawn called me.

"Yo man what's up" he said.

"Yeah what's going on dude talk to me man? How can I help you out? I only want what is best for you. So what's the problem" I asked?

He hesitated for a little while. I heard him fumble the phone like he was trying to get his words together the right way.

"Well (he started). I don't think that its right that you are spending all this time with her and you're not working with anyone else. You're not being fair".

"Well, whenever you have an album coming out don't I do that for you? Don't I bend over backwards to make sure you have everything you need for a tight album? U can ask everybody. I do everyone the same way. So, if I do it for U why can't I do it for her? I know what you're saying but your being selfish right now. I leave and now you want to say something. You couldn't say something while I was there. Do me a favor. Before you do anything wait until I come back off of the tour. Then we can talk ok" I said.

"Alright" he replied and hung up.

Shit. Through all this fun I'm having two problems (like always) they are coming to the surface. A shrink my friend saw once told me put a face with your problems. One face is not that big (Shawn). I could probably be able to take care of that myself over the phone. Vinni was a real problem. I took it to a new level … one that I'm accustomed to so I'm not scared that he is going to be furious. Just to check on my suspicions I called the hospital and they informed me I was correct. One broken are, one broken leg, four cracked ribs and his jaw is broke in three places.

Everything I had to do now would be over by then. By the time he gets better we'll be on the European tour. Then there's rehabilitation so when he comes I can take a vocation (so to speak) and we will settle the score. Maybe he won't come at all and I won't have to worry about it. We'll wait and see.

It was eleven when I drifted off to sleep. The dream I had was crazy. I was standing in front of a large crowd. I could hear the track and my shit was on. Vinni comes up from the rafters in the back, slowly making his way up to the front. I cut the music and told my security here he comes. Still moving very slowly he parts the crowd like he's GOD. Even security moves out of the way. After several attempts he climbs up on stage and starts walking towards me. The microphone in my hand becomes a gun and I point it at him. In turn he stops, holds his hands out and turns around slowly. Out of nowhere a gun appears in his hand and once he finished the turn he points the gun at my head. I pulled the trigger four times and four holes appeared in his upper body. Then he fires.

Bang ... Bang ... Bang ... Bang ... Bang ... Bang. I jumped out of bed holding myself, searching for bullet holes. Bang ... Bang ... Bang. My head of security was banging on the door. I looked around and realized that the plane had landed. I got out of bed and opened the door. He was looking at me crazy.

"What's goin on man" I asked?

"We just landed. Cool that thing off I don't think you'll need it" he said pointing to my hand.

I looked in my hand and in my grasp was my nine-mm locked, cocked and loaded. I shook my head as I walked back to the bed. That dream had rattled me. I have these dreams all the time and same thing happens, I never die.

"Your stuff is already being loaded into the car" he said.

"Alright" I replied.

I tucked the gun into my back and grabbed my suit jacked. I will take a shower when I hit the hotel. I really didn't smell so I would be alright for a while. Patricia was still groggy but happy to be on land. I can really tell she hates planes but she hates wasting time more. If we had took the bus (which I love my bus) we would only be half way here, but we're here in St. Louis with now three days of rest instead of one and a half. We could get in some shopping. So once we hit the hotel we slept a few more hours.

Dottie's aunt lives here and she has been visiting them. I might go pop up in on her. I miss my baby. Even though I miss this I can see why I left it alone. I didn't have anyone to share with. Dottie is the best part of me.

I did have a schedule to keep but one day really won't hurt me. Our cars were waiting for us downstairs but I've called Dottie to come pick me up now. I'll just drive over there.

I left the hotel and embraced the road. No bodyguards riding with me or behind. My homie Art lives in the Lou (St. Louis) and came up to the hotel room this morning. It was a long ride but we talked about his business dealings and how construction was helping him out.

The air was nice. Not too cool, not too hot, the area looked just the same back home and once we hit the suburbs it was on. We made a left on maple Rd. and followed the yellow or blue houses down to the end. The red brick house was on the end and in clear view.

We pulled up into the driveway and I jumped out before the car stopped. I ran up the steps and knocked on the door. My girl answered the door and she was so surprised to see me she pulled me into the house. Her kisses made me remember why I missed her. He Aunt and uncle came to see what was going on.

"Girl who you got up in here early in the morning" he asked?

"This is my man" she replied smiling.

"Your man" her aunt asked as she came from the front room?

Her name is Carla. If I'm Five-Eight she gotta be about five nine. For all of her fifty years she doesn't show signs of thirty-five. She had on a flower robe with bunny slippers. Dottie always said her favorite aunt Carla looks like grace Kelly and she wasn't laying.

Now uncle Rachard likes to have fun. If he had been to any of the barbeques we had he would be funniest person in the group. I can tell that he has a drinking problem though. It's only nine o' clock and he's drinking Vodka straight from the bottle. He had a medium build. What made him look stronger was he was only five-nine. If he were any taller it would make him look like a wimp.

If Carla were any closer to my age though, I would talk to her. She had a figure like a wine glass. She came over and gave me a hug. Rachard came over and gave me his hand.

"My name is Devonte and this is Art" I replied.

"Hold on. I may be sixty but I know a face. You're umm" ... He started.

"Mr. Smith" I replied.

Carla jumped up and down and realized it also.

"Oh my gosh ... I gotta call Bobby. He is not going to believe this" She said.

She darted into the back room and five minutes later there was a knock at the door. Carla came out of the room and darted to the door. When she opened it two buggy eyes peeped around the corner. Then the body of a fifteen-year-old boy appeared. He had some friends with him. She shut the door and bobby ran to hug his sister. He had a nice build and portrayed himself like a pimp.

He turned around to see me sitting there on the couch. He fell over the coffee table in disbelief. I reached over to help him up but he hopped up like nothing happen.

He looked wide-eyed at Dottie and asked "Can I touch him"?

Can I touch him? What am I; a chucky doll. I really didn't pay it any mind because I wouldn't believe it if I were in my living room either. I think he handled it very well. He looked at Dottie, and then Carla asked could his friends come in? Dottie looked at me for approval. I nodded yes because I didn't have a problem with it.

Carla opened the door and four of his friends stumbled in one after the other. I chuckled for a minute. They all stood there dumb founded. If I had a camera I would take a picture of this.

"Did you touch him yet" one of the boys asked?

"Naw. Not yet" Bobby said.

"Did he say anything" another one asked?

"Naw. Ask him something" Bobby said.

"Are you really" … he started to ask?

"Yes I am" I replied.

"Can we get an autograph" he asked?

"Sure come on" I said.

They started hi-fiving each other and grabbing pieces of paper. I signed a few then Dottie came over and sat beside me. She was smiling uncontrollably and I didn't understand why until later. I promised that I would stay for dinner but I needed some alone time with Dottie. Once we got into the car we talked about Bobby.

See Bobby was fourteen when their (Dottie and Bobby's) parents died. So it really hurt him to move to St. Louis with his relatives. Dottie stayed in North Carolina after the funeral. I know this would make him feel a whole lot better. I wonder what we are having for dinner.

LOOSE ENDS

The U.S. tour wrapped up and in two weeks we head to Paris to start the overseas tour. Still there are two things that I have to deal with. One in time and one right now.

I got to Atlanta at six o' clock and landed on my front steps by six-forty-five. Patricia went home to Wisconsin to spend some time with her family. The last part of this tour was Miami. I love Miami. I should have spent a week down there.

Shawn came to the house and was now sitting on my couch. I could tell he was upset. He felt that he was done wrong. It was my job to straighten it out. That is my thing. Besides this everything is tiptop.

Smith Inc. is putting up big, big numbers and Patricia's album is already 2x platinum. The album is so hot it will melt iron. I keep my laptop with me so I can still keep up with business issues. So the information I was about to receive is nothing new to me.

"I wanted to tell you in person that I signed a contract with Ryde records. I didn't want there to be any bad blood between us so I came here in person" He said.

"Shawn (I started) all because I was busy doesn't mean I'm deaf, dumb, and blind. I saw the interviews, I read the articles, and I got word of mouth from people inside the company. So you think you are hurting me with this. I could really care less. You felt like you had to do something and you did it. I'm not going to hold you back. I'm going to set you free. Now you can make the music you want to make. Live the lifestyle you want to live. If you call me I'm going to hang up. I don't have ill feelings. Some of the others do. So when they start saying things, doing songs, and shit. It's not me OK. Have a nice day and get outta my house.

He just sat there with his head down rocked for a minute.

"I'm sorry man" he said.

"Don't be (I said). You made a choice. I said wait until I get back before you do anything. You said OK. Two weeks ago I hear you signed with Ryde records. I'm not your friend I'm not your enemy. I used to be your associate, now that's gone to. If you could, get your car out of my driveway and keep going" I said.

He did just that. He pulled that big truck (the one he probably won't have anymore after Ryde pimps him) out of the driveway. Dottie pulled up two minutes later and parked the car. She looked depressed. I grabbed the keys to the truck and walked outside. She was there with Bobby, her aunt Carla and her uncle Rachard and some other nieces and nephews.

A smile lit up and Bobby's face when he saw me. I locked the door and put the alarm on. I walked down to the driveway and gave him a big hug. Carla and Rachard came over I gave them a hug. I went over and wrapped my arms around Dottie. She wasn't taking it too well.

Today they are going to demolish their parent's house. They couldn't stand to see it without them in it. We all piled into the car. I climbed into the driver side and started the engine. I began to pull off but paused for a second.

I was glad to be part of their future … I pulled off and the police car pulled in front of us to lead the way. The caskets were being moved to a family crest that everyone (including I) pitched in for. It was in the middle of the cemetery so no one would get to it at night (By anyone I mean thieves). First we were going to watch them tear down the house.

We reached the house in time to see the bulldozers arrive. Before the house was torn down each person went in and grabbed something of theirs to put in the room with them. After everyone was gathered on the lawn, we watched the bulldozers tear the place down like building blocks. I think it was necessary to do that. Dottie held on tightly to the vase from her mother and the watch from her father.

We were ushered quickly to our vehicles by a police officer in his mid thirties. We hit the road and soon were headed toward the edge of town. As we turned into the cemetery Dottie grabbed some tissue as Carla and Rachard sniffled in the back seat. Bobby was so glad to see me again that he didn't show it affecting him.

I could see that his expression changed once we stopped at the crest. I got out of the car and shut the door. Dottie got out next and then the back seat emptied out. I approached the crest and began to look at the construction of the crest. I ran my hand against the side and along the back. I admire the workmanship.

I was the last one to go in. I chose to go in by myself so I could let out what I had to. I walked down the marble steps to the level with five rooms ... now two of them were full. I rubbed my hands along the walls and a feeling of warmth came over me. I placed the item in the mother's room and went to adjacent room.

As I placed the item down on the table, thoughts entered my head. How many people have I buried? How many more people have to die before I find peace? Now they are watching what I do; would they approve of me seeing their daughter. I touched the casket and said ... "On everything that I am, and everything I have, I will protect Dottie with my last breath".

I walked up the steps and once I reached the outside, I shut the doors behind me.

I looked up and they were all looking at me. I don't know what they were looking for sadness, sorrow, and strength. Whatever it was I didn't have it now. Dottie walked up to me with a box. She had tears in her eyes as she handed it to me.

"Papa wanted me to give you these (she said). He wouldn't let me open it. He said you would know what to do with it".

I took the box and walked to the truck. I climbed in and opened the box while they paid their last respects. Inside the box contained a card and another box. The card read.

Mr. Who ever, I know about secrets. I have secrets too. You have to straighten up your past before you can move forward; I know that you will protect her by all means. Inside the box is a token of my trust in U. I know everything will be alright. You are just what she needs. I will always be here just call.

He took his secrets to the grave and he only shared them with GOD. I carefully took out the little box and shook it close to my ear. I removed the ribbon that surrounds it. I took a breath before I opened the box.

Inside was the most valuable possession they owned; their rings ... all three of his and all four of hers. There was another note underneath that box. I closed it and picked up the letter.

I know you know what to do with this. I know how much my daughter wants to marry you. Make something special out of these. The minerals in the gold are special. She will be able to tell if you used them or not. I know your are a loyal man and will do the right thing. Remember were pulling behind you all the way.

I tucked the letter inside the big box and closed it. I was touched. Why would he give me these? He wanted me to marry his daughter. I wanted to marry Dottie and he saw that. I pulled out the drawer under the seat and put the box in there. Dottie, Bobby, Carla and Rachard climbed into the car.

"Are U OK" she asked me as she touched my arm?

"Yeah perfect" I replied as I started the car.

We followed the police escort from the cemetery to her cousin's house. Victor was a barber turned, entrepreneurial businessman. He owned most of the business on the strip. He had a big house (not as big as mine) on the hill. He already had the barbeque set up and once the cops left (although they would be back for food) the food was on the grill.

I sat in the house and played with the computer while I made some phone calls. The first one was to Patricia to remind her that she had to be here next Wednesday, so we could leave. The second was to Chris to let him know the situation with Shawn was over. The executives were really happy about that and the fact Patricia's album (Happy days) hit three times platinum. I called Patricia and told her the news and she told me that we would celebrate next time we meet (her treat).

It seems my gamble has paid off. Now I most of all was reaping the benefits. Dottie came in the room and sat down in front of the TV. I shut off the computer and sat down next to her.

"Tell me about the accident" I said.

"I had just left out the room and they said we're going to the store. They were on the phone with me when they were blind sided by a station wagon. The impact caused the car to spin around and get hit again by a bronco. Then simultaneously they were hit from the front and the back. I heard it all over the phone I dropped the phone, jumped in my car and drove to the scene. The police weren't there yet so I saw the aftermath. (She started to cry while she explained). I tried to reach them but I couldn't move. Before I knew it the police were clearing the area".

"How come you didn't tell me earlier" I asked?

"You were working and I didn't want to bug u" she said.

"You should have told me (I said). I wanted to be here for u".

"You came right when I needed you. You have a knack for being on time" she said grabbing my hand.

She laid her head on my chest as we watched TV. Victor started to say something as he entered the room but shut up quickly when he saw that I was consoling her. He motioned that he would be outside. I was rubbing her head when she looked up at me, then kissed me. I kissed her back and I could tell she wanted to be alone with me.

"I think I should postpone the tour for a week" I said.

"Why" she asked?

"Because I can't leave you alone right now ... let me rephrase I won't leave you alone right now" I said.

"Ok then. You can take me with you. I've never been out of the country. I really want to be with you; and I am on your album. I can be your hype girl. Plus I gotta get busy doing something" she said.

"That sounds like a good idea, but I need one more reason" I said jokingly.

"I know that you're going to take me but…. we can fuck on top of the Eiffel tower" She said smiling.

"Ok. You win" I said smiling.

Second Legs

I couldn't believe what I was seeing. Everyone was at the house. I could tell Dottie has reservations about going but she wouldn't tell me. I also knew from our conversation before she always wanted to travel. I am not going to twist her arm and make her go. We are supposed to leave tomorrow. If she goes than she goes.

Patricia came into the front room and sat on the couch. I think the time with her family did her well. She was very eager to get on the road again. She was jumping all over the walls until she went outside.

It took me almost a week to relax. I still have that nightmare (should I say dream) and her father's words still are ringing in my head. I have to go back and fix my mistakes. Correct the past. That would not be easy.

I went outside to get some fresh air. The temperature was about ninety-six but it wasn't humid. I learned a long time ago to take time and smell the roses. Everything I have a came from hard work and sacrifice. Even if I wanted to give all this up now I couldn't. This is my outlet; I do have to admit popularity does have it perks.

Dottie came up beside me and pinched me on the arm. She was gleaming from ear to ear.

"I've decided to kick fear in the butt and go with u. All those girls over there might have something different than the girls over here do" she said.

"The only thing that's different is the accent and the languages. They are still fans just like everyone else" I replied.

"So why are we waiting for tomorrow when we can leave right now" she asked?

"I need some time to recollect my thoughts. I don't want to get too high. Then I won't be able to come down" I replied.

"I'll know what you mean. I used to watch you on TV a long time ago and wondered what I would say if I met you. So when I met you in the hospital I had to get closer to u to make it real for me. You replaced my boyfriend. That's why I started working all that time all the hospital. At first it was only to avoid what I was feeling. Then it became more. I wanted to be with you. You made me feel special. I never thanked you for that" she said.

"Yes you do. Everyday you wake up beside me … you thank me" I said.

We held each other that night … not wanting to let go. We stayed up all night and talked so I can happily say she was on that plane with me. That made everything worthwhile … all the interviews that I did, talk shows, everything.

She even got on stage with me. She was scared but she was never afraid to do something. I loved that about her. First we hit London. Among other places we hit were Madrid, Amsterdam. They loved us in Amsterdam. We did about three of four shows there just because the weed is legal (among other things). Patricia found a friend and spent a lot of time doing certain things in not so discrete places.

Hey it's Amsterdam. Dottie and I also did something I have never done. We rented a whole floor of the Demur hotel and fucked in every room. There were no words to describe it. We were all over the place. We even fucked right in the hallway. There we were, our shoes in one room, our clothes in another.

First she pulled off my shirt. I in turn pulled off her skirt. She ran out the room into another. I followed closely behind but stopped at the doorway. Her panties were in the middle of the floor. Shit this is fun. I dropped my pants and left them right there. I ran into the other room and my boxers hit the floor. I flashed across the hall naked when I saw her. She followed me into that room and took off her shirt and bra.

After the socks flew off it all went up hill. I wrapped her up and pushed her against the wall. I held her hands over her head as she began to purr. She spread her legs farther apart so that I could feel how wet she was. The fact that she could so anything to me that she wanted turned her on even more. She pushed my head down as she began to cum.

I prodded slowly with my tongue and tasted every inch of her pussy. She tried unsuccessfully to push my head away and then pulled my closer. I moved my tongue inside her rapidly while I played with her breasts very slowly I moved to the left breast. While I played with the pussy with my fingers, I tasted the sweetness of the left then the right breast. She was reaching for the ceiling.

While my fingers were still inside of her, I pulled her down to the floor and laid her on her back. I was ready. She was ready. We had our mind set on this. She reached down and pulled me up to her. Our eyes met face to face. She pushed me backwards and was kneeling over me before I could move.

She inserted my cock into her mouth and started to suck slowly. It took all of my will not to pull her on top of me and fuck the shit out of her now. This was her show as well as it was mine. She began to move faster and faster. It was coming. I felt it. I screamed out. She stopped and sat on top of me.

She knew what she wanted. She wanted to have my child and I wanted her to. She began to grind faster and faster. She leaned forward and put both breasted in my face as she started to cum. All I could do was let go. I couldn't hold it. She let go and I let go.

"OH FUCK" she shouted!!!!!

"SHIT" I followed!!!!!

But she didn't stop. Faster and faster, forward, backward, up and down. The world has collapsed and we were holding it up. It was all us. I turned her over and began to give it to her like she wanted. She grabbed me and held on for dear life. She let everything out. I was going to give her everything I could. Everything I had. Her body had taken control.

She began to shake. She tilted her head back and closed her eyes. She felt me inside of her pounding like tomorrow was never going to come.

We rolled from one side of the hallway to the other. She was now on top of me ... I cam three times already. I could hear her, feel her, taste her, smell her, and see her even with my eyes closed. She arched her back and moved rapidly. I too arched mine and the results were explosive.

"AAAAAAHHHHH! Just slow down. If ... you move we will have to go again" I said exhausted.

"That's what I want" she said laughing.

So back down the hallway we went on loving each other until we couldn't move.

My bonnie, that's what she is. As the shows continued the more aggressive she got. She also knew when to give up control though. We are the perfect match, untouchable. I did my part, she did hers. Patricia came on before us so she got her moment to shine. She was having fun too.

She had met a rich European in Rome and he decides to travel. She started to spend a lot of down time with him in the hotel room. I made her better on stage.

So the shows in Berlin, Biennia, Athens, and Colombo were off the hook. We were originally supposed to end the tour in Berlin, but I added more dates.

So with dates in New Delhi, Moscow, Bangkok, and Tehran among other places we were going to be busy for a while. Nobody cared. The more shows we did the more they got paid. Everybody loves money.

There was something else that was starting to press me. Vinni is probably back to full strength. He may be looking for me. In fact in know he is. I'm just waiting for him to show up in the crowd. This is my problem so I can't tell anyone. Just like he said about secrets … this is one I had to keep to myself for now.

We took a lot of down time between shows, so that we could experience the different cultures. It's a real eye opener how the things we take for granted could save someone else's life. The things I saw personally have changed my life. I see things a whole lot differently.

It seemed to have an affect on Patricia also. Her European lover left and I thought that was going destroy her but she kept rolling. She actually has impressed me. She has a resilience to go through rough things. I give her a lot of credit.

There are only four shows left and no sign of him yet. I know he is going to show up. So that I could collect my thoughts I took a little time to myself. I walked the streets of Taiwan. The people were very friendly and the kids walked behind, around, and in front of me.

It felt good to see the people that my money touches. Now these people can put a real face with the money. A little boy came up from the alley and ran all the way down the street. He was shouting something that made the children stop. They held their hands out for me to stop.

This isn't the first time something like this happened. Me, Dottie, and Patricia (Patti) have become like a close-knit family. One day we were in New Delhi and we were surrounded by a bunch of fans.

A little boy ran up through the crowd and handed me a hat. It looked like it belonged to an elderly man. I gratefully accepted the offering and bowed. I saw an elderly man in the background bow then went back into his store.

Well this kid runs through the crowd of other children and hands me a box. This is Taiwan. I'm not sure about the bomb situations here. I don't want to open this box and blow up so I asked him to open it for me. I handed him box.

He opened it and handed it to me. There was a sword inside the box. I looked up and once again an elderly man was standing in the street. I grabbed the box and walked toward him. I thought he would move toward the store but he wanted me to follow him.

I followed him into the store where there was another elderly man sitting down. He looked up and smiled then waved me on. I walked over to him uncertain of what was happening. I do wish my security was here right now. I sat down at the table and put down the sword.

He called the other man who had walked me in over to the table. The place was full of antiques and karate equipment. Kendo sticks, numb chucks and other artifacts were scattered everywhere. He brought another sword with him. The man who was sitting brushed his beard with his hand. He put one hand on the case and the other on the sword handle. He looked at me and smiled.

He bowed his head and pulled the sword out to its full length. There was writing on both sides. The other man quickly got down on his hands and knees and jumped back up to his feet. I started to do the same but was told not to. He started to read the makings on the sword. Although I was distracted by the red dragon on the case I still heard his words.

"Danger approaches. Beware. It will not come quickly but slowly. Seek the dragon for safety. (Then he turned the sword over). Vengeance is thine enemy but also your best friend. Use it wisely" he said.

He put the sword back into the case and picked up the other sword. This one was blue and black. Also this one has a dragon on it. He pulled the sword from its case. Like the other sword … both very sharp … had symbols on it also.

"The paths of wise men are many. The right one may be wrong. (He turned the sword over). Once a decision is made beware of the consequences they may be deadly" he said.

He put the sword in the case and in one motion handed them both to me. I graciously accepted them, bowed and stood up from the table. I put the swords under my arm and hurried out of the store. The street was clear except for a few kids. I walked back towards the hotel. It bugged me how the street just clear like that.

The hotel was not far from the shop. The show wasn't until tonight and the walk I took to collect my thoughts only made it worse. I put the swords in my suitcases and sat down on the bed. Danger approaches. I know what that means. I have to get my head right before the show.

Dottie came in skipping around the room. That took my mind off my problems. She came over and gave me a kiss.

"What's up baby? I went to this shop and got my nails done. Patricia went too. We had so much fun. I brought you back something. They recognized me and gave me these. (She showed off her shoes). They wanted me to give you these" She said pulled out some chopsticks wrapped in a scroll.

I reached for the scroll and it dropped. The chopsticks fell on the floor and as I picked them up. I put them together. There was the imprint of a dragon. all of these fucking dragons. Danger approaches, beware, paths of wise men. I bet the scroll says something about that too.

I picked up the scroll and opened it up. There were no words on it. There was only a dragon killing another animal. All the fables words don't mean a thing. This explained it all. I have to kick his ass. This is finished.

With my mind clear we did the show and knocked the roof off. Toward the end of the show I looked into the crowd of jubilant fans screaming I thought my enemy appeared. I looked into the crowd and through all the people, I saw him. I blinked and he went away.

Danger approached the last night in Cairo. I saw him once at the hotel, once in the audience and after I told them I would meet them back at the hotel. I followed him to the center of town. He knew I was following him. I kept telling myself that it was not time yet. I have to get him where I want him. Put the ball in my court.

I high tailed it back to the hotel and grabbed my things.

"What's wrong" Dottie asked worried?

"I'm getting out of here tonight. I'm just really eager to go. I haven't felt my own bed in eight months" I replied.

"OK let's go" she said.

Fortunately it seems everyone was ready to go so we got on the plane and took off.

"Goodbye Cairo" I replied as we left the country behind.

Dottie snuggled up to me for the rest of the flight.

BAD VIBES

I woke up the next morning with sweat all over me. I had that same dream but in slow motion. Dottie was lying next to me and Patricia ended up on the floor. By the time we got in last night our bags went upstairs but we didn't. We made it to the front room and crashed.

It was about two when I woke up. Dottie was still sleeping. I picked her up and carried her to the elevator. I pushed the button and waited for the elevator to come down. It seems like everyone was sleeping. I opened the door and stepped in closing the door behind me. The elevator stopped on the top floor. I stepped off and headed to the bedroom.

I pushed the door open and made my way to the bed. There were still clothes on the floor. I laid her down and put the cover over her. I gave Lisa's parents the other house because most of her stuff was there anyway. I had the rest of her stuff sent there after the funeral. I saw her favorite blouse.

I brought her that blouse when we went to the islands. I could still smell her perfume, but it had a different scent. It's the scent of a different life so fresh but so distant. I walked over to the closet. I pushed the doors open to reveal another room.

I walked to the rack on the left and found the box with several items they did not throw away. I opened the box and put the blouse inside of it. This is the last thing I have to get rid of. I'm ready to do that now. I put the box back and picked out a couple suits and carried them to the rod hanging over the door. They were all black. I call them my funeral suits because wherever I wore them ... someone was going to die.

I picked out some shoes and put them on the floor by the door. There were five of them in all. I kept about twenty of them. I only have these left. I will probably leave all of them behind after this.

I exited the closet and began to unpack. Mostly everything was dirty so I put it in the hamper to be dry-cleaned. I wasn't going to stay here for that long so I didn't put my luggage up. I had to get a plan together.

I closed the closet door and exited the room closing the doors slowly. My housekeeper was up. I walked downstairs to the first floor. Rosa was in the kitchen making eggs, bacon, sausage, ham, waffles, and pancakes.

I sat down at the table and grabbed the newspaper off the table. She had people helping her prepare the meal. It has been a while since I saw her. She told one of the other cooks to take over. She came over and gave me a hug. She was on vacation when the accident happened and came back after Dottie and I left.

She sat down and asked me how I was doing. We talked for a little while. She told me she went to El SALVADOR. She also told me how she heard about the incident.

"That girl spoiled you. She let you get away with anything. You need someone who is going to tell you to stop sometimes" she said.

I just loved her accent. It was so thick. It made me think of Puerto Rico.

"It took me a while to get better but everything is alright. There is some stuff I have to leave at the grave than I have to go away for a while. I don't think about her as much because I've been busy" I said.

"Are u sure that's the only reason" she asked?

"Among other things" I said.

"Where do U have to go Mr. Smith" She asked?

"I have to handle some business … some Personal business. Stuff that I can't involve anyone else in" I replied.

"It's Vinni right" she said.

"Yeah" I replied.

"Do you know how long it will take to find him" she asked?

"He's already coming after me. I don't have to. So I may send her on a vacation while I take care of him. She had a lot of fun but I can tell she is whipped. I need for you to do something for me after I leave. I need you to clear this house of everything. Move it to the new house in New Jersey. This house holds too many memories. The new house is not as huge but everything will still fit. I've already looked at the place and it's big enough. I'm going to see what Patricia is going to do. She will probably go home. Dottie can help you set up things at the new house. I will meet you back there after I'm finished" I said.

"I know about your dealings with him before. He was a very mean man" she replied.

She covered her mouth. A look of concern came over her face.

"It's ok. I know what I'm doing. I can handle it" I replied.

She smiled and patted my hand. She slowly rose up from the table and started to prepare plates for breakfast. I picked up my newspaper and started to read the reviews of the tour. They were so good I don't know why my phones weren't ringing. I folded the newspaper and placed it beside me.

Rosa places a plate full of food in front of me. She smiled once again. She knew I liked her smile and she has a good personality. She was trying to make herself feel better because she knew of Vinni's ways. She had a run in with Vinni herself.

A while back her brother got into some trouble with Vinni. He owed him some money and Vinni tried to break his neck. He was in the middle of the street kicking him. She was screaming at the top of her lungs "**STOP … STOP**"!!! I was driving my car and I stopped.

I hopped out and stole the shit out of him. Immediately his men tried to jump on me but I pulled out my gun. They stopped and picked him up and put him in the car. For someone who talks a lot of shit, he stays on his ass. So anyway, I took them both to my house to clean them up. They had pushed her around a little bit.

When we got up to the house they were amazed to see how big the house was. I didn't see the extent of the damage until everything was cleaned. I could see he had a few cracked ribs and a fractured arm. I couldn't make him move so I let them stay until he got better. She took care of him and loved the house so much, and she stayed when he left.

He comes by every now and them to take her out. Usually I'm not here. But ever since then Vinni and I have been on bad terns ever since. So he was probably crawling out of his skin, eager to get me. The same way I wanted to get to him.

By now everyone was at the table eating. Dottie was sitting next to me. Patricia was sitting on the other side of me. D and Bo went with us and were now sitting on the other side of the table. I thought this was as good a time as any to drop the news. Before I could Bo had some news of his own.

"Me and the wife are going to the rocky mountains in two weeks. She wanted to know did any one want to come along" he said.

Dottie had never been, so she really wanted to go. She looked at me for approval. I smiled because I couldn't deny her anything. She was on board and by the looks of it Patricia was on board to.

"I have something to do so I will meet you guys up there" I said.

"Are you sure" Dottie asked sounding disappointed?

"I am absolutely positive" I said smiling.

"OK" she said as a smile spread across her face.

"So what's up with the house" D asked?

"I'm going to move everything to the new house and have this one destroyed" I replied.

Dottie looked at me funny then started to shake her head. I think she understood.

"Too many memories" she asked?

"Yeah too many memories" I said.

"I wouldn't want this house either. So what are you throwing away? I want the fountain" Bo said.

"You can't have the fountain right now. In fact they have to tear it down. It's too big to move. Once they are done you can have it" I said.

"Can I get the other one" D asked?

"Yeah, you can both get one" I said.

After breakfast the party moved to the front room. I had already called the moving people and they would be here tomorrow. I went upstairs and started to pack. The only thing I kept out the box was some jewelry, and the last five black suits. I only needed two pairs of shoes. That was all I needed.

I went to every safe in the house, even the ones in the floors. I gathered up everything. It totaled up to three million dollars. I began to load the car. I put the money in a suitcase and put that in the car. I also put the suits, shoes, and the box in the car. The last thing I put in there was the jewelry.

The only thing I was going to leave with was the money, everything in the car and what I had on. I joined them downstairs and started to dance with Dottie. I could tell she wanted to do something else with me. I pulled her away from the party and into the hall closet. I closed the door behind us and she started to giggle.

"What are you doing" she whispered?

"You know what I'm doing" I said.

She slowly slipped down her top playfully. She let one strap off her shoulder then let the other one fall. He exposed breasts made my eyes cloudy. She unzipped her skirt and let it fall to the floor. Slowly she removed her underwear and began to pull at my pants. She unbuttoned them with her teeth and pulled them down viciously. She pulled down my boxers and swallowed me. Slow than fast. She didn't stay there long. She sat up on the old desk that was there. She spread her legs open and laid back.

She wanted me inside of her but I took my own pleasures to heart. I began to suck softly on her clit then began to finger her at the same time. Just like her I didn't waste a lot of time. I quickly stuck my dick inside of her and watched her move around on it. It felt good to both of us as we came together. She laid her head back.

"I really needed that" she said.

"I'm not finished yet" I replied.

I picked her up and caught her by surprise. I ripped my shirt off and put her back up against the wall. Now she was all mine and had nowhere to go. She knew it. She wrapped her arms around my neck and went with my motion. I love when she put her head back. That lets me know she's feeling it. I felt her shaking but I didn't stop. She didn't want me to. She held tighter and pumped her hips. I was deep inside of her and I began to lean back myself. She took her hands and pushed back against the wall. I fell backward on some covers that were on the floor.

She came right with me and never stopped moving. Her pussy was wet and she felt every inch of my rock hard dick. She began to moan as she rocked back and forth, while I drove my dick up and down inside her. We came at the same time.

That was some exciting shit. I went back to the party and she entered from another room. We met in the middle of the dance floor (front room). If this world was mine came on the radio. I held her tight and she felt that I was still hard. She moved closer to me and put her head on my shoulder. She rocked to the music and to the beat of my heart. I listened to her breath and any thought of Lisa was erased. I had Dottie on the brain and no one could stop it.

This was right. There was no other way. Not even Lisa did this to me. Emotionally, physically, spiritually, every part of me craved for her. She was what I needed. Didn't let me do wrong (the stuff she knew about) but let me do naughty things to her. I knew I had to do this now.

Everyone went to sleep around ten o' clock. The house was as quiet as it had ever been. I walked around the halls looking for signs to tell me to stop. Don't destroy this house that used to hold love. Truth be told it was old. The other houses were rebuilt and added on to a year ago and were still new.

There was mildew on the ceilings and the walls were screaming at me. GET OUT ... GET OUT. Yeah it was really time for me to go.

I took the box Dottie's father gave me and put that into the car with the other stuff. I knew the next time I leave this house will be last time I was going to see my kids before my trip so I packed a few (two) sets of regular clothes and threw them in the back. I was prepared to face my enemy. This is my happy ending and that's what it will be, so help me GOD.

SECRETS

It seemed like every room I entered reminded me of her ... some happy thoughts, others sad. The only thing left to do is move the car. I crossed the front room and went down the foyer that used to have a statue in it. It took them two days alone to move that.

I walked slowly to the driver side and climbed in. The car roared to life with a turn of the key but the car didn't move for a minute. I thought about calling it all off, but it was; it is too late the balls already in motion.

I put the truck in drive and parked down the driveway so that the machines would have enough room to get through. I got out of the car and walked back up the steps. I walked slowly like I was trying to hold on to something. When I reached the steps I sat down.

There was nothing left. Even the pool was drained. Too many memories held this house up and as long as it stood I could never move on. I knew that. I also knew the longer I stayed on these steps I would never leave. It was a relief to see that white sedan followed by five bulldozers and a wrecking ball and crane. I couldn't have been happier.

I handed over the keys to the house and walked away. That was the last time I would go in there. The last time those walls or floors would speak to me. The last time her voice would call out to me (I'll always be with you). I made my way to the truck and climbed in. I couldn't leave until it was done.

Minutes later the wrecking ball cleared a large portion of the third floor while the bulldozer tore into it from all sides. I guess they got tired and blew it up from the inside. Everything crumbles to the ground and they started to move the debris out of the way. It was through. It's over so I thought.

They cleared a path where the garage used to be and there in all the debris was a brown door with a lock. I drove up and parked quickly. I jumped out and pulled out my gun. I run up to the door and swung quickly to my left so the bulldozer wouldn't hit me. All action stopped as the workers ran over to see what was going on.

There was a door in the floor. Who put it there? It wasn't me. Could Lisa have done this? If not her who? I told them to stand back and I blew the lock off the door. I swung it open and was surprised at what I saw.

Someone had built this. I was away a lot and she never went anywhere else. I walked down the steps to the floor and found a light switch. I walked to the back of the room, which was nothing but a bunker with concrete walls. It wasn't this that got me. There was a radio and answering machine.

I walked over to the answering machine and all the messages were for her. I pulled out my cell phone and called the house number (which should be off). It was, but once the answering machine was cleared new message was being recorded. I could hear a phone ringing in the corner. I ran back still dazed and found it. Before I could say anything a voice started to speak.

"Hey Lisa this is Vinni. I just wanted to let you know that I'll be waiting for you in Champagne Beach next week. Meet me at our hut."

Shit. What the fuck was going on Vinni and Lisa together … at Champagne Beach? I will be there and kill both of them. I took the tape and snatched it out of the machine. How the fuck could she do that? Everything started flowing through my head. Were they sleeping together? I'll just have to ask.

There were a bunch of tapes on the table next to the machine. I grabbed all of them and left. I put the tapes in my car and grabbed some dynamite. I looked at the men as they looked at me. She already knew where to be so how was she getting calls?

I ran back down stairs and started pressing keys on the computer. I found the forwarding number and wrote it down. I spread it out from the back of the room to the front. As I laid down the last stick I stepped on a panel in the floor. The whole room modernized, metal cabinets came out of the floor and settled into place.

Heavy artillery, money and other electronic equipment lay everywhere. Was the original plan to kill me? I grabbed a couple of guns with ammunition and stuffed them in duffel bad. Then I lit each stick one by one, ran out, and shut the door behind me. The bulldozers had already moved back. I put the duffel bag in the car. I was so pissed off when It did go off I wasn't phased. The door blew into the air and everything in that room evaporated.

I used to miss that bitch. I would die for her. Shit, I almost did. Did she set the whole … Naw? She wouldn't do that. I hit the pedal and was off. My mind is buzzing right now.

I drove to the freeway underpass and the box I was going to put by her grave went toward making a beggar can fire a lot bigger. Fuck her. She didn't know it yet but her ass was going to get it too. Since this is still fresh I have to think of the right way to get her. If she is still alive how could I find out?

I looked down at my phone and thought to myself (what if she answers at this number). No it's too easy. I dismissed the thought and parked in front of an old worn down factory. There was a jewelry store in the front but I went in the back. I knew everyone from a long time ago. It was time to catch up.

I had made up a list of some jewelry I wanted made, so I was melting down the old stuff and making new. I grabbed the box of jewelry and the rings Dottie's father left and went in. It was dark, but when my eyes adjusted I could see perfectly well. I had drawn everything I wanted. It would take about a week to complete so I had time.

There was an older gentleman, kind of chubby with overalls. He was bent over a melting pit crafting something.

"Hey big shot" I shouted as I approached!!!

Whatever he was working on he was finished because he put it in a cooling machine. He turned around and once he saw who I was he ran up and gave me a hug.

"Boy … I ain't seen you in a long time. Where you been" he asked?

"My wife died and I've been in mourning. I need you to do me a favor. Melt all of this down for me. Then I need you to make the designs on the paper and send it to this address when you're done" I said.

"It's already done (he said). I need to show you something man" he said.

He took the boxes and put them in his drawer and locked it. Then he took me to the front part of the store. Uninterrupted by the clerks he opened up one of the cases took a ring out and closed the case. He told me to walk with him outside.

As we walked outside he handed me the ring. Now as my eyes fixed on the ring I noticed something. The same ring I was holding was the same ring I put on Lisa's finger. I wanted to cry I was so pissed.

"When and where did you get this" I asked.

"She came in yesterday. She told me you two got a divorce and she didn't need it anymore. She just left it. She didn't want any money or anything. She wanted it destroyed and when I did it to call her at this number in Champagne Beach" he said.

Champagne Beach ... shit I gotta think of a plan.

"Do you have the number on you" I asked?

"Yeah she left me a picture" he replied.

It was her. The phone number was the one I got off the computer. I'm starting to get the picture. I still need a little bit more information.

"Where is she staying now? Is she in New York" I asked?

"Yeah she's at the Days Inn on Fifth Street. What do you want to do with the ring" he asked?

"Tell her you destroyed it ... but I'll take it. Do me a favor. Tell me if you see her again. Call me. Don't tell her that I was here" I said.

"Ok" he said.

I started to walk away then turned around abruptly. He put his thumb up to say ok man. I stuck one finger up and he nodded. I got in the car and started to drive. No destination planned I just drove and ended up parked by a phone booth.

Why would I stop at a phone booth? The thought had me perplexed. It couldn't be true. I should just pull off and give up this silly notion that she is alive. What if she is alive?

I had to know. I got out and walked slowly to the phone booth. I needed evidence. I grabbed my cell phone and dialed Bo's number. I guess he had me on speaker because I could hear everyone.

"Hello" he said.

"Yo ... it's me. I don't have much time so turn down the radio and don't say anything alright" I said.

"Cool" he said.

I put the cell phone up to the receiver, put a quarter in and dialed the number. The phone rang four times and the machine picked up.

"Hello you have reached Lisa & Vinni, please leave a ... Hello ... Hello ... is anyone there? Hello ... Vinni if that's you get down here. I'm ready to start this thing with you. If you forgot the address it's four-fifteen firebird lanes. Hurry Up" she said.

I hung up the phone and put my cell phone to my ear. I began to think Bo hung up but he thought that sounded like Lisa too.

"That sounded like ..." he trailed off.

"Yeah" I said finishing his sentence.

"What are you going to do? If you need my help call me, matter of fact where are you? I'll be there in an hour" Bo said.

"No. This is my problem. I gotta fix it" I said.

"It's my problem too. I gave her some money before the accident then she disappeared" he said.

"How much did you give her" I asked?

By the way he paused I could tell it was a big amount.

"Three" he said.

"Three hundred" I asked?

"Three hundred thousand" he said.

"I will call you when I get where I'm going. What about the trip" I asked?

"This is money. The trip can wait or the girls can go alone and we'll meet them. Chris and D are going so they'll be ok" Bo said.

"I'll call you then" I replied.

I got back in my car and drove to the Days Inn. I found out which room she was staying in. I got another room. I paid for in cash under another name and went in. It looked like they redecorated from the last time I was here. The room still looked the same.

One bed, one dresser and two lamps on each side. The TV was small. I needed a bigger room. I would get it later. I called Bo and told him where I was. All this running around made me tired so I took a nap.

My cellular phone woke me up about nine hours later. My friend Ronald (from the jewelry store) called. He told me I would be able to pick my stuff up Thursday and Lisa was on the way to the hotel. I'm thinking someone who doesn't want to get caught would stay away from where a persons at. I remembered one important detail. I hate New York so I was never here. So she must think she is safe. She is about to find out she is wrong. I have a mind game for her.

I rose up out of bed and headed for the door. I was halted by the sound of a key in the lock. I hid in the bathroom but when no one came in I poked my head out. I put my head towards the door and still heard rattling. I immediately looked out the peep hole. I didn't have to look for her. She was right in front of me.

She underestimated me. I should kill her right now. She was wiggling the key. She got frustrated (like she always does) and went downstairs. I cracked my door to make sure she was gone. I struck my hand out and snatched the key out of the door. I went down the hall and caught the elevator. I got down to the lobby and was headed to the front desk. I stopped short when I saw her at the desk.

"I would like room five-zero-zero-two (she said as she handed the clerk some very crispy bills). Also my room key is not working" she said.

"Bring the old key back ... but for now take this one" the man behind the desk said.

She went upstairs to the bar. She sat there for a while. The first floor was the lobby. Gold and White trim over a Black background. The second floor was the bar and restaurant area. The remaining floors are rooms. The Fifth floor is a pent house suite. So she did have Bo's money. He was on his way up here.

I very quickly commandeered room five-zero-zero-three and moved away without being noticed. I went to the bar and ordered a martini for myself and a rum and coke. I swallowed my drink and told the bartender to give it to her. Once he moved I walked out of the bar and into a back chair.

The bartender whispered something to her and pointed where I was sitting (which was now empty). She looked and shock came across her face. She jumped up quickly and rushed out of the restaurant. I followed behind. She got on the elevator and some little kids on a field trip cut in front of me. I stayed in the back of the elevator hidden by seven kids and three adults. They went all the way to the top. She wasted no time getting off the elevator.

She ran to the room, opened the door, and closed herself in it. She made a mistake though. While she was pulling it out the kids ran her over, pushing her into the room. The door shut behind her giving me enough time to pick up her key and get in my room before she could open the door. I had her right where I wanted her.

I had a micro camera that I put over the door after I left the room. I ducked in case she was looking out the peep hole. Now I knew that she loved roses. So I took some (two) out of the vase and laid them in front of her door, knocked, and took the steps downstairs. I had to get her to leave so I could follow her. If she felt that it was safer at the "Beach", then she would go there.

I got down to the lobby and Bo had arrived. I waved him on and we caught the elevator up. Now that my dog was here the cat is in trouble.

I thought Bo had come alone but D was with him. I told them about the situation. I showed them the ring. I played the recording that they heard also.

"I want my money man" Bo said.

He has been having a fit since he got here.

I got keys to both of her rooms ... we can leave tonight. The only problem is that I have a package that won't be ready until Thursday" I replied.

"So we wait" D asked?

"Yeah ... we wait" I said.

"I'm going to sleep" he said.
"I needed some downtime anyway" I replied.

HUNTER

We've been waiting for three days and nothing yet. My package is ready for pickup and my patience is wearing thin. So we are going to have to push her to Champagne Beach sooner than she planned. She's been in room Five-zero-zero-two. No one left. No one came in. No noise. Just silence.

I'll have to scare her away. I grabbed my keys and went to the truck. I told the fellas not to move until I say so. They want her as bad as I do. The trip was turned into a spa resort for the women so we can take care of business. With the girls out of the way payback was in effect.

I met up with Ronald and he gave me my merchandise just the way I wanted it. He had some vacation time coming up so he followed me in his car. He wanted to fuck her up for lying to him. So now we come up with a plan. We went back to the hotel and met up with Bo and D and got it together. Either way we had to get her moving.

Bo, D and Ronald waited across the street downstairs. Ronald called her and told her the ring was destroyed at the same time I knocked on the door. She seemed to be so happy until she opened it. It was like a scene from fright night. She almost dropped her glass but squeezed it so tight that I saw her veins popping out of her arm.

"H … H … H … Hello" she said stunned.

"I was wondering if you saw the cleaning lady. I spilled some food on my rug and they still haven't sent anyone up" I said.

I never saw a black person turn whiter than new white sheets before but I'm seeing it now. She started gasping for air. Now I couldn't have her dying on me … then she couldn't lead me to Vinni.

"Well I'll just try again later" I said walking away.

That did the trick. She flew out of the room with her shoes in her hand. She even tripped on the way to the elevator. I took off down the stairs to my room on the fourth floor. She stepped off the elevator and dashed into her room. I ran into mine and grabbed my briefcase, then took the stairs down the rest of the way.

Two minutes later she flew right past me in the lobby. She turned in her keys and begged the valet to hurry with the car. I turned in my keys and went out back. D was waiting in my car and when I got in he smiled at me. I know what he wanted to know. She got in her car and took off. Me, D, Bo and Ronald took off after her.

I picked up the phone and called Ronald. He picked up very eagerly.

"What's up" he asked?

"I think you should get back to the store in case she goes there and remember you haven't seen me" I said.

"Lisa is not going back to the store to see" he said.

"I remind you … we're talking about Lisa" I said.

I saw his car turn around and go the other way.

See she needed confirmation like I did.

"So when I tell her I haven't seen you she's not going to leave" he replied.

"I bet you two-hundred she does. The winner buys the food on the road" I said.

He hung up the phone and we followed Lisa around town. Sure enough she went to the jewelry store. She was panicky as she jumped out of the car. We pulled up almost after she did so when she looked we had already killed the engine. She left her cell phone on the hood of the car by accident. She hit the door running hard.

I took the cell phone and opened the back. Behind the battery I put a tracking device and a bug. I put tracking devices all over her car. Some so obvious they would rub off on her when she sits down. I put the cell phone in her car and closed the door. Ronald had just told her he didn't see me because she was a bit calmer. That was until she saw me.

"Ronald what's up man (I said ignoring her). Who is your friend? She reminds you of Lisa a little bit don't she. Oh, I'm Mr. Smith and Lisa was my wife before she died. I miss that girl so much. Hey Ron you got a minute. It was nice meeting you miss … miss.…" I started.

"Williams. Mary Williams" she spat out.

I walked Ronald out to the car and we got in.

"I think you should leave your car here" I replied.

"Man you saw her face. She is not going anywhere" he said.

No sooner had he said that, she ran out of there high speed, jumped in the truck I bought her and took off.

"I want my money" I replied as Ronald, D and Bo looked at me and started to laugh.

We followed her to an auto parts store in Pennsylvania (where she slept and woke to find her tires slashed). She spent some money and brought a car.

"Bo (I asked) how much do you think she has left"?

"How much what" he asked?

"Money" I said.

"Aw shut up Man. You're always rubbing shit in" he said.

"I'll pay you back every cent as long as you do one thing for me" I said.

"Anything" he said.

"Tear all of Vinni's men a new asshole" I replied.

"It's already done" he said smiling.

Since there were four of us (because we dumped one car), we took turns driving. Two rested while one keeps the driver company. While she stayed in the hotel we slept in the car with the windows down. We used the hotel rooms to take showers and eat sometimes but that was it. Anything we bought on the road as far as clothes we left in the room. I was hunted; she failed to take me down so now I'm the hunter.

There were things we did to keep her going farther and farther. Some things we shouldn't have done because we have women at home, but she pissed me off so I did it anyway. Hey they all did it to so we all have a lot to confess to our women. It is all for a purpose. If we didn't do the little things she would go back to New York, and we didn't want that.

We've been on the road for hours and days. She is so desperate to get away from whose chasing her she even drove on the wrong side of the road. Once we hit North Carolina I knew what was up. She stopped in this little diner. I was hungry anyway.

We took a seat in the back of the diner. I was playing a hunch and after we ordered our food, it paid off. Vinni came walking into the diner and sat down across from her. I could tell they haven't been intimate. When he reached for her hands she pulled them away. He wanted to but she wasn't ready. She was like that with me.

They talked for a while and seemed to be arguing with each other. He slapped her and she covered the bruise with her hand. I wanted to help her but then she hit him back and said "don't you ever hit me again". He mouthed the words I'm sorry. They stayed there for a couple more minutes. That was long enough time for us to finish another round of pancakes. We went out after they did so that we weren't seen.

Why am I worried if their having sex or not. She tried to play me. I still didn't want him touching her like that. I don't want her back but she won't be with him. She fucked over the wrong man.

She jumped in the car and he jumped in a separate car. They took off in opposite directions. I could give a fuck about him. I put a tail on him anyway. I want to know where he's going.

I wanted fucking payback and I'm going to get it. I don't care about anyone else's motives but my own. She is going to pay for everything she has done to me.

"I think she may stop in Atlanta. She has people there that she trusts. We can't let her stop" I said.

"We can't control her driving man" D replied.

"So we have to somehow keep her going" I said.

The conversation shifted from that to the fact she tried to give me the shaft. When you hurt someone bad enough love turns to hate, gratitude turns to disgust, loyalty turns into a prison and respect turns to fear. I looked in the mirror as we're riding on the freeway. I don't recognize myself. It feels funny but I'm very comfortable here. I could be shooting people for no reason at all and not feel a thing.

I need to calm down. At the rate I'm going I'll probably kill her with my car and keep rolling. My prey is in my sights and all I have to do is follow it until it stops. That's what she is to me, a thing. It's have no business on this earth and it's my job to dispose of them.

I'm seeing flashes of red right now. Cars zooming in and out … Red and Blue … that's it. My target is blue and it's three cars ahead of me. In my wreck-less mode I almost hit the car in front of me. I moved quickly to the other lane. In a second, I skipped over the two cars in front of me and was right behind her.

My emotions would have to wait. I wouldn't be satisfied with the bait. I wanted the hook. I wanted to string his ankles to a ceiling fan and turn it on high. I can think of a million ways to kill a rat or a snitch. This one has to be special.

As I'm contemplating the best way to get him I realized I pulled into a truck stop. I saw her just sitting. No … she was sleeping. I don't think she was going anywhere near her family. Not for fear they would be put in danger.

She wouldn't go near them because if she did she wouldn't meet Vinni at Champagne beach. I don't think it was a sexual thing at all. As I reviewed the tapes I got from her hidden office and the bug. I sense it is more of a business opportunity. He wanted it to be something more.

The thing is … we were running out of land. Two more days to go and my revenge will be complete. I wanted it to be over but I was going to take my time dishing out punishment. The floods gated were open and the well was flooding.

Bo in the driver seat replaced me and I lay down in the back. I haven't been to sleep in two days but I feel like I just woke up. Ronald was having a ball. He bought a bunch of cameras and had used about four of them. He just started on a new one.

I got out of the truck and went inside. I ordered some food and had it to go. Everyone got out and stretched their feet, legs and arms. Our location was about one or two hours from Miami. Depending on if they take a plane or a boat I got them. They're trapped. I know she's going to meet him somewhere, but where I don't know.

I walked past her car and peered inside. She used to look so beautiful when she slept. She slept with her mouth open. I say slept instead of sleep because I don't know her anymore. I never did know her and that's the fact that hurts the most.

I would like to stuff her head in a meat grinder. Shit, if Vinni was here now I could just go home. I could smoke both of them and walk away. No regrets, maybe I'm being too anxious. I should get her attention by knocking on the window. No … my revenge is at hand.

I moved away from the car and handed the fellas their food. As we sat in the truck and ate we tried to devise a plan.

"Where in the hell are we going" Ronald asked?

"I have a pretty good idea but I'm not sure" I replied.

"Can we at least clean the car before it starts to stink" he requested?

"Sure" I replied.

After we finished eating we crossed the street to a little used car wash. We broke in and grabbed some cleaning supplies. Bo started to wash the outside of the vehicle. Ron (Ronald) vacuumed the inside and somehow put a new car smell in there. It wasn't that bad when we started but after it was cleaned you could tell a different. D put the sparkle on and I threw on different license plates.

I received a call that Vinni had rented a boat and planned to take it out tomorrow. He was staying at the Snails Hotel near the Marina. He was going to pick up the boat around eight. I hung up the phone. That is useful information.

I told the fellas the news and we all jumped into the truck. As fast as we got over there you would think we were police. I parked the car and turned off the ignition. I got in the back seat and Bo took over the wheel. A short time later we were on the road again.

I feel tired, but my eyes won't close. Every time I close them they open back up. Am I dreaming or is this real. The hallway is dark and there is not light. There is nothing on the walls and I can't feel the floor. I think I dropped something. I bent down to pick it up but my hand went through the floor. I kept my balance and made it to a door that opened on the bottom, but was separated from the top.

I took one step and fell down to a level where I was blinded by light. On one side was Dottie in white under a blue sign flashing the word … love. On the other side there was Lisa underneath a sign that said hate. Vinni was there also. He was smirking at me under a sign that said kill. I was all by myself. It was my choice.

There was a gun in front of me. I reached down and picked it up. My aim went directly to Vinni and without thinking I pulled the trigger. I aimed the smoking gun at Lisa and squeezed the trigger. Dottie screamed out "Stop" and the bullet disappeared. I turned quickly and stared at her. She said "thank you" and disappeared.

I woke up and shook my head. Sweat was pouring down my face. I managed to sit up in the seat and saw that we had stopped at the Marina.

"What's going on fellas" I asked?

"She stopped" D said.

"Did she get out of the car yet" I asked?

"No not yet" Bo answered.

Just then I saw a boat pull up and she got out of the car. The boat pulled up to the dock and was roped off.

"Time to go gentlemen.... get your stuff" I said.

"Where" they asked?

"Champagne Beach" I replied.

"Lets go then" Bo said.

Caught In The Trap

I put on one of the black suits to mark the beginning of the end. Dai de los mortos (day of the dead) was about to begin. We passed by several islands. Ronald has had his head over the side all day. He didn't tell me he was seasick. I should know these things right?

My boat has three sections. The main steering compartment and lounge area on the second and bedrooms and everything else is downstairs. Black wall-to-wall carpet with Red fluorescent bulbs illuminated the room. The large theater sofa stretched from the bar to the bedrooms with a mirror on the ceiling. I designed it myself.

My boat trailed theirs from a safe distance. Through my binoculars I could see them toasting champagne. I could kill them now, but I need them to see it was me. I need to see her face. I want to inflict so much pain, emotional, mental, and physical that if she picks up a dollar her hand will let it go.

I began to lean back when I saw something new. I've been all over the world and I never saw this island. They were heading straight for it. Nothing but palm trees and sand. It's beautiful. I took my time turning up the speed to keep up with them.

They changed course to the back of the island and we followed. On the other side there was civilization and a port. We pulled in and docked. It was to hot for the suit but I had to wear it. They docked on the other side.

Vinni had about four or five bodyguards and she had about three. That's eight shots alone. I grabbed the suits and we followed them up a narrow pathway to a remote part of the island. Through the woods and rough, the path we were on got wider until a big cabin appeared in the clearing. I ducked down as they entered.

This is perfect. Now they are in and they are not getting out. I looked at the suits I had in my hand and got an idea. I told the guys and they went along with it. Somehow we had to get their attention.

I moved closer to the cabin and lit all the suits on fire. One by one I threw them at the bodyguards. One of the guards caught fire. He screamed as the fire burned his skin. The others tried to put him out but he was already dead.

Vinni came running out of the house. There was a frightening look in his eyes. He saw his men badly burned and one dead.

"What the fuck is going on" he screamed?!!!

"Bobby's dead. Somebody set something on fire and he caught it. It came from over there" he said as he pointed in the opposite direction.

The fire got him turned around, good.

He looked nervously in that direction. What was he thinking? Lisa came out and saw the fried man on the ground. She screamed and ran back in the house. Now I had their attention.

"Let's come back tonight. Well change clothes and finish this" I said.

"Alright" they replied.

Now I know why they love Champagne Beach. I love it to. They don't ask questions. You can come and go as you please. The best reason is because they serve the best food that you've ever tasted. We had plenty of time.

I set up mini locating devices so that I would know if they left. This is the first meal in a week that I haven't had to rush through. Plus I was enjoying the scenery. I wouldn't mind living here. I should buy the next island. Ronald was looking for some sexual pleasure.

So with the girls at the retreat for the week, we thought we would have some fun. There was this club called The Sipping lounge and the party they were having was jumping. So the fellas and me bought some new clothes and were dressed to impress. Immediately there was circle of girls surrounding us. I was having so much fun I didn't notice they left the house.

I looked up and they were on the other side of the room. I pointed over and told the guys. They were trying to get some tonight. I had something else in mind. It was getting kind of late because it was dark. I called the fellas over.

"Look if you wanna fuck then get the number because we gotta go" I said.

"Why man" Ronald said?

"If we don't get into that house now then we never will" I replied.

"Can they come with us" he asked?

"Yeah but come on" I said.

Why not? It wasn't my place. I didn't take long to get there because we cut through the woods. I picked the lock on the front door and busted in with my gun drawn. The whole house was gigantic. I loved the wood panel ceilings. They made good hiding places.

Vinni doesn't know how to appreciate a house like this. The pictures, (all of him) had to be taken down. The furniture plaid and corduroy shouldn't have made it to the warehouse. I walked into the kitchen and found the dullest knives I've ever seen. It had a country feel with poultry all over the place.

I opened the refrigerator and grabbed the milk. It wasn't open so I grabbed it by the handle and set it by the stove. I made my way upstairs. The fellas were getting along nicely (if you know what I mean) so I walked the long hallway to the main bedroom. I didn't expect what was in there.

This room had Lisa written all over it … from the white curtains, to the satin sheets. I admired this room. The dresser, bed set was to die for and the mirror closet was a nice touch. I was headed to the bathroom when I heard a noise.

I grabbed my gun off the bed and hit the hallway. The fellas had finished and were sending the girls off. I shut the door behind them and looked out the window. They disappeared down the path and out of sight.

"I'm glad I got that" Rodney said.

"Yeah any longer and it would have effected me permanently" D said.

"What about you man" D asked?

It took me a while to answer. I didn't have a complete plan but something was forming.

"I got an idea. When they come back ya'll get the guards outside, kill them I don't care. I will take care of Lisa and Vinni. That's all me. Just don't question it ok" I asked?

"I got you man" replied Ronald.

We were interrupted by a lot of noise coming from outside.

"Ok. Once they get here the guards go out. Remember anything goes" I said.

They all nodded in agreement. I hid behind the couch and pulled out my gun. I had the perfect view of the door. D was hiding behind the wall of the dining room. Bo was hiding under the stairs in the hollow section. Ronald was on the other side behind the living room wall.

It seemed like forever. There was so much noise outside; I made up my mind to go get them. I stood up and started to walk towards the door. I pulled out my other gun and crept closer and closer. I was almost there when I heard keys.

Oh shit. I ran and dove over the couch. The door flew open and Lisa and Vinni came in. He told the guards to stay outside. He thinks tonight is his lucky night. He didn't know about my plans. Tonight is the night. He will not see tomorrow. I promise that.

She went upstairs. Once she was gone and Vinni was headed my way.

D, Bo, and Ronald headed outside. My attention turned to Vinni. I know by experience no matter how much noise was being made she wasn't coming downstairs.

Out of the corner of my eye I saw Vinni headed toward the kitchen. I turned on the beam and pointed at the milk. I was taught to be patient. He stood in front of the sink right where I wanted him. He had no idea what was about to happen.

I pulled the trigger and watched the bullet go through the milk, then his hand. I jumped over the couch and landed on the table where he could see me. He turned around holding his hand and fell when he saw me. He tried to run but my next shot (which hit the counter) stopped him in his tracks.

He had never seen me like this and he was scared shitless. I never saw myself like I am now. All the rage I built up turned me into another person. I was looking at myself as I moved and acted. I wanted him to move but he wouldn't.

I moved closer and he took off. I shoot at him but missed the first time. I still held position and caught him at the stairs. Bang, Bang twice in the leg. He fell down to the floor grabbing his leg.

"Hey I'm sorry. It was her plan she wanted to do it" He screamed!!!!

"How long ago was it setup" I asked?

"For about a year … She wanted to pay you back for picking your career over her. Plus she wanted your money. She said she would have poisoned you if you ever came home" he said.

"Why would you help her" I asked.

"Once I found out the truth about my inheritance I wanted to kill you too" he said.

I grabbed a chair out of the dining room and grabbed him by the shirt. Just then Bo, D, and Ronald came in smiling covered in blood.

"Have fun" I asked?

"Hell yeah" they answered.

"Help me get this bitch upstairs" I said.

We got upstairs and I put the chair down in the bedroom Lisa was in. Bo and D tapped him up and left him right there up against the wall. I wanted to make him kill his self. Knowing how much he wanted her and I hated I would make him suffer.

I didn't even pull my pants down. I sat her up and she did it for me. She was drunk so she would have sucked a horse's dick. She always did give good head. I looked over and Vinni is going crazy in the chair. He didn't like that.

With only me and him in there (and her) this worked to my advantage. The curtains were drawn so he only saw the shadow. That was enough I turned her around so he could see her face as she took her time. I pulled out my gun and stuck my gun in her face. She was still sucking me off. I cam all over her.

"Open your eyes" I said.

She almost choked when she saw me standing there. I moved back and pulled my pants up. She looked at Vinni. He looked like he was getting ready to tear up. She put her hands over her face and her face in her lap.

She began to cry. Her tears didn't faze me anymore. She stood up and moved towards him. He had his head bent down. She wanted him tonight and I ruined that. Good … I wanted to.

"I wouldn't do that if I were you" I said holding the gun to her head.

The door began to open. I backed up against the wall. Boom, the door came off the hinges. This dude was big. Vinni looked up and started to squirm around this dude is six-three to my five-eight. He didn't see me over by the wall. Lisa started to say something but I pointed the gun at her to shut her ass up.

All of a sudden he came charging at me. I opened fire and emptied the clip. He was still standing. Boom … Boom … Boom. D, Bo, and Ronald came in taking shoots at this dude. Finally after twenty shots he fell.

I reloaded and walked over to Vinni. Took out my knife and put it up against his neck. His body stiffened up. I could see the pain in his eyes. I crushed him, which was my plan. There was only one thing to do with him.

I walked around slowly, gun in one hand, knife in the other.

"I'm going to let you go, because you're really a bitch and you don't deserve my bullet. Second it takes a better man to walk away. I'm tired of this life so you're free to go" I said.

The reaction was novel. The look on her face turned into a smile as I cut the tape behind his head. I then proceeded to cut the tape around his ankles. After I did that I stood up and started to pace the space between him and her. I pulled a coin out of my pocket and flipped it.

"Vinni you pick one and Lisa you pick one. I wanna see how my luck turns out" I replied.

Vinnie picked heads and Lisa picked tails. I gave the coin to D and asked him what it said. He told me heads. I walked back over to Vinni and put my gun to his head.

"Don't move until I say so. I mean it or your brains will be on this floor" I said.

I cut the bindings from his hands. He didn't move an inch. I backed away enough so that he couldn't get the gun. D, Bo, and Ronald were looking at me crazy. I put down the gun and said go ahead.

He started to move and was half way across the room when I moved behind him and pulled the trigger. His brains blew out the back of his head. The body fell to the ground and my gun was still smoking.

She got down on her knees and started to cry. She held him in her lap and cried. I didn't feel sorry for her at all. She deserved everything that happened but it's not over. She still has hers coming.

She stood up like she was ready to charge at me. I held the gun to her head and she stopped. The fear in her eyes was jumping out of her body and she fell back down to the floor. I walked up to her and put the gun to her head.

"I'm going to ask you some questions, and I want straight answers OK" I asked?

"OK" she said.

"You have some money you borrowed. Where is it" I asked?

"It's all in the closet. All three hundred thousand" she said.

He opened the duffel bag and brought it in the middle of the room and put it down. I looked at him and the smile on his face said it all. I chuckled and looked back at Lisa. She stood up and walked towards me. I let her kiss me one last time, and then I pushed her away.

"Take me back with you. We can start over from the beginning" she said.

"I'm sorry. This is the end. By burying the past I can start over fresh. I already saw your grave so to me you're already dead" I replied.

I took the gun, put it to her head, and pulled the trigger.

AFTER EFFECTS

The last thing I remember is the phrase (straighten) up your past. The look of (what's the word I'm looking for) hope. Like she really cared. It was too late because she took me to a point where I didn't. I took the ring out of my pocket, wiped it off and slipped it back on her finger. I'll probably get it back when I claim the body so fuck it.

Sure enough they gave it to me when I claimed the body two days later. I walked in the room. It felt like an icebox. The bottom door was open and the doctor was staring at me idly. I nodded and turned to leave. He covered the body up and closed the drawer ... then the door.

He walked over to the desk and picked up a piece of paper.

"Mr. Smith, (he started) you don't seem too upset" handing me the piece of paper.

"We've been through a lot" I replied.

"Yeah most couples do. If you got something hold on to it, you never know when it's going to end" he said.

"Yeah" I muttered walking out of the metal doors.

I went upstairs and collected her belongings, some car keys, the ring, some boat keys and a locker key. I walked out of the hospital and jumped into the car. Bo looked at me. I wasn't even paying him any attention.

"What are you going to do with that stuff? I thought it was over" he asked?

"We are going home tomorrow but something's need to be done" I said.

"What do you mean" he asked?

"People, her people, have to believe she was already dead. They bury her and if they know about this stuff then they will know she was still alive" I explained.

"Did you see Vinni" he said?

"Briefly … had to make sure" I responded.

He started the engine. First stop was to go to the house and destroy that. I had to erase any existence of her life after death. It was a long boat ride back to the island. I didn't want to return but I had to. From the moment we stepped on the island the mood had changed.

I felt as if the king and queen were gone and never would return. I had the envelopes in my hand and started to walk across the beach. The weather was not too hot so I took my shoes off. A native of the island came over to me and told me to follow him. Only Bo was with me, besides Ronald had to … Well wanted to go back to work and D would be our alibi in case the girls go back early.

We jumped in the jeep and sped off into the woods. Through all the thick brush I could see the house. The driveway was being dug up. They must have been looking for something. I jumped out of the jeep. The native and Bo followed me to a gigantic hole that had formed. Deep inside the hole there was a chest with a lock. They pulled the chest out and carried it to the jeep.

I looked at the lock awkwardly and reached into the manila envelope. I blew the dust off the lock and started to put the key in. A whole lot of noise interrupted me momentarily and the native went to see what was happening. I looked at the chest, then at Bo, then at the chest. I turned the key and a series of clicks went off.

I cracked open the chest enough to see tons of money she had hidden. I don't think he knew about this. Then again maybe he did. What he didn't count on were the police watching him. These weren't police. These were the protectors of the land. They knew a box was buried there and they wanted it out.

The native came back telling us to take it all away from here.

"Poisonous … take it away. Do not bring back" he said.

I locked the chest and threw the key in my pocket. I was taking it anyway. She owed me. They started to refill the hole. As the native was talking to me, it turned out they hated them (Lisa and Vinni). They were glad to see them gone. I walked over to the car and got in. Bo got in also.

I jumped out of the car and ran to the back of it. There was a cliff in back of the house.

"GET OUT OF THE CAR" I YELLED!!!!!

Bo got out and I jumped in. I rolled down the window. I told him to wait in front of the house. I put the key in and took off. I flew down the freshly replaced driveway and out the front yard. I sped down the dirt path until I got all the way down the hill. I stopped the car at the bamboo shack.

I picked up two stalks of bamboo and jumped back in the car. I put it in gear and hit the petal. Turning the car around was easy and I was headed up the hill doing seventy. All the natives were standing in front of the house talking when I zoomed into the front yard. I put the bamboo sticks between the gas petal and the seat. Bo looked at me crazily and followed me as I drove the car around the back.

I aimed the car to go over the cliff and got up on the headrest I jumped out of the car and landed on the soft ground just as the car took flight. It seemed like forever. The car cleared the beach and two minutes after the drive started, the car disappeared completely under the water. Bo started laughing at me because I was on the ground.

"You crazy as shit" Bo said.

All the natives started to clap and went back around the house. By now, everyone had seen my anger had gathered around the house. A slow chant began to start.

"Burn it down … Burn it down … Burn it down … Burn it down"!!!

I was on a roll. I ran into the house and grabbed some paper, pulled out a lighter and started to light it. I started upstairs and worked my way down. Surprisingly the place went up pretty quickly. I came out of the front door and joined the others.

Everyone was cheering. I actually began to feel better and the only thing left to get rid of is the boat. In fact I feel like a million bucks. I think that I could actually fly right now. As the house burned down so did my last connection to her. I began something new.

I could return to Dottie a change man. I can give her everything I couldn't before. I am now a free man … person … being. I am going to walk away. What happened here never happened!

I walked back to the car and got in the back. It was like liberation. Bo got in and the native that was with us jumped in the car. He put the key in the ignition and the car came to life. He turned the car around and stared back down the hill.

It was like a parade. We were going five miles per hour. Everyone who came up the hill were now singing and dancing behind the car. I was happy that I could do that for them. I would do it again.

I don't know how long it actually took to get to the boat but by that time, word had reached the beach. They were having a party. I wondered what Lisa and

Vinni did to make people act this way now that they are gone. What ever it was they don't have to worry anymore. I had freed them along with myself.

Bo convinced me to stay for a while before we left. It would be cool to accept any gifts they had to offer I could take them back to Dottie. I had one more thing to do first.

I had to sink the boat. That was the last piece. I took the keys and ran to the boat. I didn't see a raft on the deck so I went down below and found it. I went down into the engine room. I grabbed a fishing spear and began punching a hole in the floor. After several minutes of trying, water started to enter the room. I made another hole on the other side and one by the door. This baby is going down.

I ran back up to the deck and put the key in the ignition. It came to life but I forgot to untie it. Fortunately, Bo came over and untied it when I went below desk. I didn't pull off too fast because I didn't need to go out that far. Bo ran to the other boat and started it. By the time I reached my destination he was coming to meet me.

He went around me and came on the other side. I went below deck to punch more holes but the cabin was already starting to fill up with water. I went back up and threw the raft down before closing the cabin door. I jumped on my boat and Bo took off back towards shore.

We watched as the boat went under. All of my problems were now gone. Erased, I had accomplished what I had set out to do. After many years of trying my past is now just that, my past. The trash was taken out and the burden was lifted. Bo had been through everything I had almost. He knew it was over.

This is our island now. We are the kings of the island. I started to think though how can you rule something you don't own. I would be as bad as they were. After the celebration I would leave and never come back. That was the right thing to do. Leave it with the natives of the island. The chest was put on my boat so we could just push off with no problem.

I sat back in a lounge chair sipping on a drink, which contain coconut, gin and something else I couldn't pronounce. I've been thinking about how Dottie would love this place. I may bring her here once but that's it. That won't be any-time soon either. I learned a valuable lesson. Never again will I be so blind to believe something that isn't.

If my experiences have taught me anything it's that no matter how much money you have trouble will follow. I also found out you can't pay problems to go away. They will be a pain in your ass until you shit.

We've been partying for hours and it's really time to go. I gathered the keys and untied the boat. It seemed like Bo didn't want to leave either. Bo climbed on the boat and we started the journey back to civilization. I didn't want to go too fast because we didn't want to miss any sights.

The money in the chest was the last thing on my mind but it was the first thing on his.

"What are we going to do with this money" he asked?

"Beats the hell out of me" I replied.

"How much money you got left" He asked?

"Two grand … the rest is gone" I said.

"We need to spend some" he said.

"What we need to do right now is put this money in duffel bags and dump this chest" I said.

"Let's get on that" he said.

We started to put the money in duffel bags so it wouldn't look suspicious. We filled both bags half way. I stopped the boat because there was something else in the chest. I lifted up the panel on the bottom and there were three or four guns, passports, and other important documents. My mind started spinning.

I don't need this I'm done. If I keep any of this stuff I haven't learned anything. I looked up and his eyes were saying (why not it wouldn't hurt though) right?

I grabbed the chest and dumped it over the side without a second thought. It made me feel good, like I had a chance to choose at last. I flipped the chest back over and looked inside. There was another compartment. I pulled the cardboard up and took the letter out.

It was addressed to me. I threw the chest as far as I could into the water. I started the boat up and pushed the throttle forward. I really didn't want to open it but I had to. I had to think before I did it.

I probably should open it. No I got a better idea. I ran down to the deck and put the letter in the water. By the time I pulled it out it crumbled in my hand. Now I will never know what she said. It might have said she loved me or she hated me.

It really didn't matter because Dottie and I have no secrets. She keeps me straight and I let her be her freaky self in the bedroom. That's how our relationship works … with everything out in the open.

I had a thought but was interrupted by my phone ringing. I picked up on the second ring.

"Hello" I said.

"Hey Boo ... What's up" Dottie asked?

"It's good to hear your voice beautiful. How is the spa? Did you think of me" I asked?

"All the time ... I want to have some fun when you get home. I'll be home tomorrow. Will you be there" she asked?

"If I gotta hi-jack the plane I'll be there. I miss you baby see you" I replied.

"See you too. Smooches" she said.

Smooches ... she has been hanging around them socialist to long. I hung up and put the phone back on my hip. We were close to shore so I slowed down and taxied into the marina. I grabbed the two bags and the shoebox. It was time for me to get home. I'm clean now.

I flagged down a cab and jumped in. Bo got in behind me. I know Chris got everything held down at the office, but Dottie was getting into the front office mode", herself. The first flight to New Jersey was leaving in ten minutes. I ran up to the counter to buy tickets but they were sold out. I gotta get home.

"Hey ... you need a ride" the voice asked?

I couldn't believe it. Matt was here. I ran over to him and gave him dap.

"Yo ... I need to get to New Jersey can you help me" I asked jokingly?

"Yeah ... I got a plane outside with your name on it" he said.

We walked outside and my plane was sitting there smiling at me "I missed U too" I whispered under my breath.

"How soon until take off" I asked as we boarded?

"Whenever you want" he replied.

"How about right now" I asked?

He nodded in agreement and in five minutes we took of on our way to New Jersey.

I sat up in the cockpit and thought about Dottie as the clouds flew around us soon we would be on a beach together with no drama. Finally everything is right. I'll keep telling myself that. Everything is right, everything is right.

A New Life

I'm home. The place looks great. I couldn't have designed it any better. Dottie isn't her yet but she is on the way. She should be here in twenty or thirty minutes.

She will probably want to know what happened on the trip. What should I tell her? I want to tell her the truth, but the truth might hurt. No the truth with hurt. She probably wouldn't understand.

It seems that people understand the person they want to understand. I am three people ... one funny, two serious, and three mean. She may understand the funny side and the serious side but when she saw the mean side before she didn't understand. So why should she now.

I just want to be straightforward with her. Let her know how I feel. I want her to marry me, but I want her to marry all of me ... every single part. It's a package deal. U can't throw away one part because you don't like it.

The blue carpet in the front room really sets off the white curtains. The high ceilings were really a selling point for me so now that they had white streams hanging from them I was in love. The whole floor has blue carpet. Of course they have to have a dragon on them. They were spaced out all over the carpet in every room, except mine.

I'm going to explain the thing about dragons and me. I am a Leo, but my Chinese symbol is the dragon. That's why the dragon means so much to me. It's a part of me; always will be. I made my way to the kitchen. The sink, dishwasher, cabinets, free-range stove with digital sensor touch controls, and plenty of counter space lined the walls. The center unit was a large flat surface used for making salads and cutting stuff. I looked in the refrigerator and grabbed a bottle of Gatorade.

I closed the door and headed upstairs. I looked for my room. I peeked in one that was painted white, with black carpet; another room was pink with white carpet and another one that was blue and white, with blue carpet. I kept looking in rooms and finally came to a room that had the door closed. I opened the finally found my room. I walked in and fell straightforward on the bed. I could have fallen asleep on those black satin sheets.

I almost did when I felt someone plop down on the bed next to me. I tilted my head to see who it was, and a very soft pair of lips landed on mine. It could only be one person. My baby was here. I rolled over and pulled her on top of me, she did not resist me.

I kissed her sweet lips and she melted on top of me. We wanted each other the same way. She pulled down my pants as I peeled her shirt off of her. She was hot. She was ready. Her nipples were hard and it was my job to take care of that. She could tell I was hungry for her also.

She didn't waste time and climbed on top, inserting herself on top of me. It's been to long. She wore a skirt on purpose. Her body moved up and down against her will and my body reacted without mine. We moved in the emotional current that our bodies had made with each other. All I could do was put my head back and enjoy this feeling.

Instead I put my eyes on her … her body, her rocking motion, her eyes. Those beautiful brown eyes … I was going to bust. She knew it. She pushed me farther and farther towards that edge. She rose up as I was about to release, then got back on and started to ride. I released as she released. We came together.

"That's what I came here for" I replied after we finished.

"I want you to take advantage of me" she replied.

I jumped up and stripped off all of my clothes. I went into the bathroom and turned on the shower. Warm water started to flow out of the showerhead. I went back into the room took the rest of her clothes off. I wanted her now. There was no more time for play.

I picked her up and put her on top of me. She threw her arms around me looked into my eyes. I looked into hers and there was something there. I carried her into the shower. The water made her more erotic than she already was. With her back against the wall she fed off of me. She grabbed onto the empty towel rack and began moving her hips rapidly. I couldn't handle it.

Her eyes alone drove me crazy. I wanted to drive her crazy. She let go of the towel rack. I put her down and bent her over. She put it out there a little bit farther. I was up in it and she was pushing it back to me. She needed me.

"I want you inside me ... I need you inside me" she screamed.

"I want you to have my baby" I screamed.

"I want you to fuck the shit out of me" she screamed.

That's exactly what I did. I fucked the shit out of her. After we finished I washed her and she washed me. I put on my robe and lay down in the bed. She joined me and we fell asleep in each other arms.

I haven't slept in my bed in two week but it felt like a month. This bed never felt so comfortable. I take it that she liked the spa. I woke up about six in the afternoon. I put some clothes and went downstairs. She was in the kitchen making her favorite dish.

I missed her cooking. When we were on that island all I wanted was some lasagna. That always hit the spot. She put the right herbs in there. Rosa left to go to the store. Since, Dottie was cooking now Rosa could spend more time with her family, but she didn't have to leave permanently.

I liked the way she sauntered around the kitchen. The marble tile matched the counters and drawer fronts. From an angle I could see what was under her skirt. She knew the spot so she stood there just to tease me. She let her freaky side show when it came to me.

Everybody came over that night. Patricia brought her family over, D and his girl, Bo and his girl, Ray, Rick, Chris, Art, Dottie's family. While I ate the lasagna, the barbeque was going outside. It was good to see everyone having fun. I only wanted the best.

The best part about it is there are no phone calls; no one knocking at the door, no (I need you) messages. Everything was peaceful like it should be. This is the perfect time to propose to her. If she says no, I will feel like a total fool. I have a very strong feeling that she won't. I just got to run it down to someone.

"Rene could you come with me for a minute" I asked?

"Sure" she replied.

She followed me up to the room. I shut the door and pulled out the box. She was standing in perfect position. I opened the box took her hand and asked her to pretend she was Dottie. She was puzzled but she went along with it. I got down on one knee and asked the question.

"Will you marry me" I asked?

She almost lost her breath when I asked the question. She almost died when I showed her the ring. She was stuck for a good minute or so before she yelled out yes.

"You are going to ask her to marry you" she asked?

"Yes. Did you like the approach or should I change it" I asked?

"No, the approach is fine. So is that ring. How many karats is that" she asked?

"Its twenty karats with a gold trim in a platinum setting" I said.

"Would you marry me? I wouldn't mind wearing this" she said.

"I know you wouldn't. Do me a favor and don't tell anyone" I said.

"Who else knows" she asked?

"Nobody except you" I said.

"When do you plan on doing it" she asked?

"Tonight" I replied.

She was surprised but she hugged me. She told me if Dottie didn't marry me she would. She wouldn't mind being Mrs. Smith. She wouldn't mind wearing that thing either.

"That's a lucky woman" she said as she walked out the door.

I know for a fact Rene couldn't keep a secret like that for long. That's why I told her … to put pressure on myself to do it. I had to act fast. This had to be done tonight.

I went to the closet and picked out my best suit, the powder blue suit with the blue gators. I took the jewelry that I had made and laid that down on the bed. I put the ring on the bed. The other rings I put them in my night stand.

By the time I got downstairs everyone was still outside. I stepped outside and caught everyone's attention. I stepped on the basketball court. I wasn't worried about the suit because I could buy another one.

Rene was looking at me eagerly. I remembered what she said and laughed to myself. The DJ was playing T.I. so I waited because I like that song. I grabbed the microphone and asked the DJ to cut the music. I could see Rene was about to scream.

"Could I have everyone's attention please? Dottie could you come up here for a minute I asked?

She came up to the front puzzled. She stepped on the basketball court and stood in front me. She was wondering why I called her up. Apparently everyone else was also. This was going rather quickly so I decided to continue.

"I want to ask you something very important. This will change your life as well as mine. I want you to be sure before you answer. I want to spend the rest of my life with you. You are my life, my world. I am nothing without you. You mean everything to me" I said.

I bent down on one knee.

"I want you to be my wife. Will you marry me" I said.

I put the ring on her finger and she almost fainted when she saw it. It was huge to me so it must be gigantic to her. I think the rock on her finger put a block on her brain. Carla stepped up and said something to Dottie. That snapped her out of her trance.

"Yes, I will. I will marry you" she said.

I stood up and brushed myself off. She put her lips into mine and wrapped her arms around my neck.

"I love you so much" she said.

"You know I love you to baby" I replied.

"Girl let me see that ring" Carla said.

She was pulled away by her girlfriends and the guys surrounded me.

"You sure you wanna do this dog" Chris asked.

"I've never been more serious about anything in my life. She is the one. I'm not ever going to let her go. We are connected in more ways than one, I said.

"She's fine as shit too. If you didn't ask her to marry you then I would have taken her from you" Chris said.

"Keep your hand off my fiancée. Y'all need to get married to y'all girls for real and stop playing" I said.

"I will handle mine and you handle yours ok. I saw her first anyway. I just let you have her" Chris said jokingly.

We all started to laugh and after the girls started to move away the guys started trickling over to see the ring. They came back telling me how big it was and that they would have to top that when they got married. I know most of these guys are never going to get married.

Chris was envious so he asked me to help him out.

"Look, I've been trying to ask Christie to marry me for a year. What should I do" he asked?

"Get her alone and ask her. Say how you feel. Make sure it comes from your heart. Just be real and she should accept it. If she doesn't you have a choice to make. The right one will come along" I replied.

"Thanks man. I gotta go but I will call you" he said.

He rushed out of the yard, through the house and out the front door. I really had to talk to Dottie. I had to tell her. I grabbed her arm and whispered in her ear "we need to talk". She followed me into the kitchen and sat down. I didn't waste anytime and got straight to the point.

"I have to tell you about what happened" I started.

"Whatever happened, I don't want to know. You did what you had to do. Leave it at that" she said.

"OK" I replied.

"Now let's go back outside" she said.

We want back outside hand in hand.

"Just promise me one thing (she was saying). No one will ever bother us again".

I nodded my head. That part I could promise. Anyone who thought about it before when Vinni was alive was thinking twice now that he was dead. They all know I killed him. No one had a doubt. Dottie knew it. She knew I killed Lisa to. Like she said I did what I had to do. It was necessary ... maybe not all of it. That didn't matter to her. What mattered is that she had me and I had her".

As she moved through the crowd all eyes were on her. It's her moment in the spotlight. People were crying and the fellas were trying to beat me up because of the ring I gave her. The upside is that everyone is together, happy.

"I want to make a toast" Dottie said.

That got everyone's attention. I loved her voice. I even loved her whisper. I started to make my way to the front of the crowd and joined her. She handed me a glass of champagne. The smile still hasn't left her face.

"This is to the rest of our lives. May they hold as many blessings and good things as my future will hold?

Everyone started laughing and took a sip of champagne. She wrapped her arms around me and made a private toast.

"This is for us let nothing come between us" she said.

She glanced at the ring then back at me.

"If you like that, wait until you see the wedding ring you're gonna get" I replied.

"Oh I love you" she said.

"Right back at ya" I said.

THE WEDDING DAY

Yes … she said yes. I still don't believe it. I've been married before but that wasn't a real marriage. I can't begin to tell you what that was. That was Convenience. There was nothing else to it … the married word meant nothing. This is the real thing … no more lies. When I'm out of town doing business … I really am.

Dottie even went with me sometimes. Between meetings we went to amusement parks and museums. All the things that we couldn't see over in Europe and the Middle East we were seeing now. It's amazing how much you miss when you don't slow down.

All she can talk about is the wedding day. We set it for August. It's the first of May and we just returned from a three-month trip. It was actually a seminar for the company where we gave out goods and services to promote product endorsement. There was a lot of down time in between so we explored places lots of people haven't seen.

She woke up on after the first day back and her family (who had their house burned down) was in the front room. I put them up for two reasons. One … you have to take care of family and two … they wouldn't have to fly in, they would already be here. They've been here for two months and have already started to make plans for the wedding.

We hired a new cook named Betty and she is a fine replacement to Rosa who visits occasionally. She stopped by with her brother to wish Dottie congratulations. While she was here she made her famous omelets just the way I like it. It felt really good to be home. I really meant that.

Dottie wasted no time jumping into the planning mix. After breakfast she started to discuss (with her family) where she wanted to get married. It really didn't matter to me because I wanted her to have HER wedding. As I sat on the couch I could see and feel her excitement.

I rose up from the couch and went into the back yard. I have a beautiful view of the coast. I think this would be the perfect place for the wedding. If the wedding isn't here this is where we renew our vows. I may bring that up to her later.

I walked around and joined in a game of basketball that was going on. I didn't have a care in the world. For the first time everything was going right. It's been months since the incident on that island and even though it's on my mind it's still in the past. I also know that she had to be thinking about it. I still try to figure out how she knew.

I figured that she knew why I was in the hospital. So I would take care of the whole situation or any that arose. Maybe she didn't care. I personally had to find out. On the other hand I saw how extremely happy she was and I was not going to fuck that up.

After the game was over, I grabbed a bottle of water and sat down by the pool. I saw something shiny by the side so I went over to pick it up. I was pushed in from behind. Good thing I took my shoes off. To play it off like I meant to get in, I swam to the other side and back.

After I emerged Dottie was laughing at me with her hand out.

"Oh that's funny huh" I said laughing?

"Yeah" she said.

"It wouldn't be if you were in here" I said.

"That you'll never find out" she said laughing.

Then I reached up and grabbed her out stretched hand and pulled her into the pool.

"AAAAAHHHHH…. I'm gonna get you back for that one" she said after she emerged.

She swam over to the other side of the pool and back (just like I did) and joined me by the steps. It wasn't that hot but the water was very refreshing.

"I really needed that" she said pulling her hair back.

When she turned her face to the side the light hit it at the perfect angle. She was an angel. My angel … Sent to deliver me from my own ways. She succeeded where no one else did.

All I could do was stare at her and admire her braveness. Yeah she knew. I know it now. For us to be together I had to finish a job that started long ago. For me to be whole she did what she had to do.

"What's wrong" she asked interrupting my thought?

"Just thinking" I said.

"About what happened when you met with her" she asked?

"Yeah" I said.

"So what happened" she said.

"I killed both of them" I said blankly.

That's all I remember about that night. Everything else is foggy. The way I killed him and the way I killed her. It's funny what your mind let's you remember. She must be disguised with me right now.

"All long as it's over … that's all that matters" she replied.

"I knew you wanted to know" I replied.

"I just didn't want to badger you about it" she replied.

"I really do appreciate that. So where are we getting married" I asked?

It took her a while to decide on what to say.

"If you haven't decided that's ok" I replied.

"Nooo … it's not that. I want two ceremonies … one public and one private. Is that too much? How does New York Times Square sound to you" She asked?

That was a great idea. It could be the biggest wedding ever. For the private wedding we could do it on the beach in bathing suits.

She was eyeing me funny waiting for an answer. I already had one but was wasting time on purpose.

"I love it" I said.

"You do" she replied?

"Yes. We can put it on the jumbo screens and everything. You set everything up if you need my help let me know. That's only on one condition" I replied.

"What's that"?

"I get to plan the private ceremony" I replied.

"OK" she said jumping up.

She went back in the room with her family and began planning (The Wedding). I went up into the room and began the simplest private ceremony ever planned. I could see it in my head. It would be made in heaven.

White doves would be perched up above the altar. Everyone would wear bathing suits because after the wedding we were going to have a pool party. I have two rings for her that would be combined into one once the ceremony is finished. I know she knows what she's doing because she's been planning things before I met her.

I could tell after a few weeks that she needed some help, so I asked Pam to help her with anything she needed to make it work. Dottie really appreciated it.

Together they got everything up and running. I could tell it was really big when she asked for a second assistant. Sure why not.

My wedding was planned to the point that the caterers already knew where to come. I changed my mind and cancelled the caterers. Why pay when we could cook for ourselves. I asked Donald Fruzenburg (the legendary cook), to come up with a menu. I gave him everyone's allergies and three hours later he came up with a five-course menu that would please everyone.

See if New York Time is twelve pm that Honolulu time is seven am. We could do both in the same day and didn't have to break a sweat. Everything was set up, date and time the plane leaves. Everything was coming through on her end also.

August the tenth. The day is approaching rapidly. With three days left everyone woke up and prepared to fly to New York. The mood was quiet but exciting. Some of her family was scared to fly, so they left earlier. That didn't dampen her mood because this is her day. This is her week.

The drive to the airport was not that bad and before we could blink we were at the airport. There was a little problem clearing customs, but they let us pass and said they could watch. I don't know how word leaked out but there was a crowd in front of the terminal. Dottie and I waited for everyone to go through and then we walked, hand in hand through the crowd. She really enjoyed it.

The clerks checked out tickets and let us pass. As we walked down the tunnel she put her head on my shoulder and that's where it stayed for the whole flight. From take off to where we landed. We are so comfortable with each other … two peas in a pod not to be separated.

The plane landed and everyone piled into cars we had reserved in front of the airport. While we waited for the bags to be loaded into the limousines the conversations varied from cooking ingredients to Lingerie. Finally after what seemed to be several minutes we pulled off. It took forever to get the hotel but that gave everyone a chance to catch up. Some people haven't seen each other in years.

My best men are D, Bo, Art, Shawn and my son Deion. Chris did not want to be one of my best men. He wouldn't tell me why. Dottie's bridesmaids were my daughters, Lakisha, Andria, her sister Carla, Patricia and her friend from back in the day, Diamond. All of us were in the limo together.

He interacts really well with people. I love that about her. She was talking to Carla as the motorcade pulled up to the hotel. We started piling out of the car and claiming our bags. They were taken immediately into the hotel and up to our rooms.

Dottie got out and grabbed me by the arm. I was talking to Bo and she was talking to Carla but she still held on to me. We finally made it to the elevator.

"Oh … my gosh is it really you? I've seen you on TV. I'm your biggest fan" the girl said.

"No I am. I even got your named tattooed on my butt" her friend said.

"We're just visiting from Connecticut. Can we get your autograph please" they asked?

"Sure" I replied.

They pulled out a piece of paper and I signed it. I gave it to her and smiled at them.

The other girl asked me to put my autograph on her chest. She pulled down her shirt and handed me the pen. I began to give it back but Dottie tapped me and whispered in my ear "I was young once too", I signed my name and one floor later they stepped off the elevator.

"You weren't offended by that" I asked?

"I'm going to be your wife so no … that doesn't bother me. I used to be like that too … Impressed by the fame and glamour until I grew up. To them you are very, very popular, hot and everything else. To them they dream to meet you. I already have you. I'm fine" she said.

We made our way to the room and when we opened the door I was amazed. I didn't know the Richland Hotel was like this. This is my first time in this hotel and I wanted to stay low key. Pam told me about this hotel. She would be here in two days to set up with the other assistant.

Personally I wanted to spend as much time alone with my Doll baby because we can't see each other before the wedding. I was on my way down to the front desk when I saw the same girls and another female. She couldn't believe I was standing in front of her. She looked like she was going to lose her breath.

"My daughters told me they saw you" she said.

"Well here I am" I replied.

"Can I have your autograph right here" she asked pulling down her shirt?

I signed my name and gave her back the pen.

"So what are you doing in New York" she asked?

"I'm getting married" I replied.

"I would love to come. Your last album brought me together with my husband. My name is Rhonda. These are my daughters Tiffany and Felisha" She said.

"I'll tell you what. Be in Times Square on the sixth and there will be seats under the tent for you" I replied.

"Thank you" they said.

I wasn't expecting Pam so soon but she stepped on the elevator.

"Pam, let me ask you. Some fans of mine want to come, could they get a seat under the tent" I asked pointing to the three ladies?

I didn't know if there was a tent but there's one way to find out.

I got off on the main floor and gave some instructions to the front desk clerk. I handed him some envelopes and walked away. As I walked away I saw him talking to the housekeeping crew. I feel like I'm the king of the world. Soon I will have my queen.

The day passed too fast. I knew if we were separated by our respectable parties. They began the pre-marriage ritual of bachelor and bachelorette parties. I didn't get too trashed because now my plan is in motion. I had to stay sober for this. This is going to be a rough night.

Finally the day is here. I make Dottie my wife today. I can hear her in the other room. I missed her so much last night. I held my pillow and imagined it was her. I wish they would hurry up with this.

The whole street was blocked off. I saw a huge tent in the distance as we approached. The family was already seated. The crowd cheered as I stepped from the car. The groom's men and my best man walked the bridesmaids and the maid of honor up to the front.

I slowly walked up the isle, taking time to make eye contact with everyone. I took my position on top of the stage. I see why she needed help. The white tent was so huge it covered the whole street. I was surprised how she put this together.

She pulled up in a horse and carriage. As she got out white doves were released into the sky. She had on a white gown with a train of twenty-four feet. It took four people to hold it. She was more beautiful than I ever saw her before. She slowly walked up to the stage and stood beside me.

We said our vows and everyone applauded as we exchanged rings and kissed. That kiss took me back to when our lips first met and when she opened her eyes she was Mrs. Devonte Smith. She started to laugh and closed her eyes as everyone cheered. So we climbed back into the carriage. She had a gleam on her from nothing could be replaced.

We were on our way to the airport. She thought we were going to the hotel but my plans were in effect now. The motorcade followed us to the airport as adoring fans waved us congratulations. Before long we were on the runway. I stepped out first and helped her down. She threw the bouquets and a fan wrestle it from someone else, and then held it up with no shame.

I saw my now number one fans right in the middle blowing kisses. The bags were already on the plane and we were the last two to board. Even the one's who hated the flying weren't going to miss this reception. Shrimp and Lobster amongst other things was on the menu.

"Where are we going" she asked?

"It's a surprise. Do you trust me"?

"Yes I do trust you" she said.

I need to borrow this for a minute" I said pointing to her ring.

"You just put it on my finger" she fussed.

"Yeah … but its part of the wedding plans … I promise when you get it back you are going to love it" I said.

"Ok I trust you" she said.

She slipped the ring off her finger and handed it to me. She made me promise she would get it back. Phillip my jeweler came up and I handed him the rings in my hand and the other half in the box. By the time we got to Hawaii all three rings were combined into one. What wasn't eatin on the plane was carted off and moved to the beach directly after we landed.

We shuttled in the vehicles to the hotel. I got the ring back and in a couple hours she would have her wish. We got married at three o' clock in New York. The flight was a couple hours flying nonstop so by the time we hit the beach it will be three pm in Hawaii. She didn't understand yet but she rolled with the punches.

I left her a note in the room while I got changed.

Put on your bathing suit under your white dress. This is a part of the surprise. You have to trust me. Pam will lead you to the destination.

About an hour has passes and all the guests are seated mostly people close to us. This is a very private occasion. A couple of people noticed the ring was missing and asked her where it was. They were clueless ones. Everyone else knew that I had it. I walked out to the podium and took my spot.

When she appeared the music started. I could see her smile under the vail. This is what we wanted. The Hawaiian breeze blew and we faced the ocean as we exchanged vows. She gazed at me and smiled. I didn't think this could get any better. That was until she saw the ring.

A crystal clear forty karat diamond in the middle with twenty karats going around the band, all set in a platinum frame with little specks of gold on the inside of the band. I could see the happiness in her eyes. She gave me the longest sweetest kiss. Tears of joy started to run down her face as she threw her second bouquet.

"Can I have everyone's attention please", I shouted. Take off your gowns and suits because the pool is now open for business. There is champagne and food at the pool area have as much as you want" I screamed!!!

One by one … after the clapping stopped; they started to strip out of their clothes. She watched as the birds were released and wiped her eyes. She slipped out of her gown and we walked hand in hand to the pool.

"I told you that you would get this back" I replied softly slipping it on her finger.

"My great grandma and grandpa's ashes are in this ring. The way the light shines on it I can tell. How did you get them" she asked still wiping tears away?

"Your father said two things to me. To use them in both rings, (I showed her mine) and to straighten up my past" I said.

"You did both. Now what about the past again" she asked?

"I can't worry about the past" I'm looking at the future" I replied.

I grabbed her hand and we jumped head first into the future, our future, with a big splash.

THE END

Everything is great now but I found out a few things after I had a chance to really settle down. When Lisa was shot she was wearing a bulletproof vest. One of the bullets went through but the doctors pulled it out. They sent her home then set up a dummy for the coroner. She paid them to say that she was dead while she recuperated at home.

To make the tests seem real they burned up the body. So when D, Bo, Shawn and Art saw the urn with her name on it they assumed the same as I did. To make it seem even more real to me she sent her family to visit and invite her to the house. She knew that I wouldn't come to the house because I didn't fuck with her peoples like talking about it. She was hoping on the off chance that I would so she could finish the job.

She had another plan to try to get me by using David, but that fell through when Vinni found out that he wasn't any relation to David. That's why they teamed up. It turns out that if I was in New York … like I was in North Carolina she would have been poisoning my food everyday. I could have been dead in a year or so. Good thing I stayed away right?

Since I didn't go over to the house she had to come up with a different plan. She probably would have put one in my head. She wanted to see my face when I died. When I caught her by surprise on the island she was really shocked. Not because she wanted to suck his dick but because she wanted to see my face when I died.

She knew that she was going to die instead of me. She knew that I would have no mercy no matter how much she begged. She had to try it anyway. I should have seen it all before. I think that my anger had me blinded. I should have left her in that fuckin warehouse to die.

That's the catch. I wouldn't have been in the hospital and met Dottie. If I went to the house and found her alive I would have killed her whole family for lying to me. I would have been in jail and any future that me and Dottie could have possibly had would have been gone. I actually haven't spoke to Lisa's family at all since I left the hospital.

Even her brother was in the dark and I don't have the heart to tell him that I really killed his sister. He separated himself from that side of the family. They tried to reach me to get to him. Eventually I changed all of the numbers that I had and put a block for their number on the office phone. They stopped trying to call me last month.

I wish that I hadn't. I would love to tell her that I killed her cunning daughter. She wasn't anything but a capital B.I.T.C.H. anyway. She didn't deserve to breathe the air that she breathed. I hardly think of her anymore. I spend most of my time thinking of what I want to do to Dottie anyway.

The good news is that Patricia is in the studio recording her second album. She has handled the transition nicely and is getting really serious about somebody. Would you believe that? Guess who she is dating? Chris.

They are pretty much inseparable right now. So while he runs the record company I take care of the other business that needs to be fixed. A couple of trucks needed repairs and one of the shipments didn't make it to its destination. After I made a few calls everything was cool. There is another problem I have though.

The local gangs were tearing up some of my tenants shops. I called in the Black Dogs. The Black Dogs are a group that I formed that really didn't have a purpose. That is until now. They solved that problem quick fast and in a hurry.

The next time they tear up the cement at the new apartment complex they will find seven bodies of people that should have known better. They will find seven more wearing cement shoes in the bottom of the ocean. That is if the fish haven't gotten them first. Word got around town for those who didn't know. That was the last time anyone did anything that could get them stuck in hot water.

They gave me the top game mark for my album. They said it was inspirational. We just signed a new artist named Fire. She is on tour and is about to drop her first album. We met her at the radio station where we hold weekly battles over the radio.

She was an intern. The reigning champion was waiting for the challenger. He hadn't shown up yet and Symphony (Fire) said that she wouldn't mind subbing in. It was time for the battle and he still was not there so she stepped in.

In my opinion she tore that girl up in two bars. I signed her to a deal right there. I was so impressed that I forgot the other girl's name. Dottie had to remind me. There is still more to the story though.

What I love about her is her work ethic. She writes a new song everyday. When she comes back we are going back into the studio with some people that want to work with her. She has taken to Dottie as a daughter would to a mother. She even stays at the house with us. My children are the brother and sisters that she never had so she is part of our family.

Her parents died two years ago and she's been out on her own ever since. She was only twelve then. Once social services picked her up she was moved around in the system for two years. She ran away and resurfaced that day at the radio station. That is the day they found her.

She was in the guardianship of the state of California for going on three weeks when Dottie and I adopted her. She slept so peaceful that night that it shocked me. We felt that she deserved the chance at a normal life. Everyone does. I had to give her that chance.

Plus me and Dottie felt that her talent was too pure to be wasted. If she had stayed in the custody of the state then she might be lost in the system forever. We couldn't allow that to happen to her. You can mess up a kid like that. She is in France right now so she flew back to rest for a few days.

So with a huge block of business cleared up I can concentrate on the music side once again. I gave David back everything that was transferred to me after he left. My name is still on everything just in case the law tries to seal his assets. We did that as a precautionary measure.

I put Dottie's name on everything of mine for the same reason. Just in case they pull a slick move I put the kid's names on there also. So now even if they try to freeze Symphony's assets they will be shit out of luck because she is covered to. You gotta protect your shit … you can't be too careful.

On another note Deion is getting married to his high school sweet heart. They have been dating for five years and feel that they are truly in love. They're getting married in April of next year. In my estimation he has become quite the business man I thought he would become.

He started his own company called The Goliath Corporation. They do construction and job training for construction experts. They are all over the United

States. For a small company that's pretty huge. There are currently fifty-five locations and they are still growing.

Even my daughters have surprised me. The oldest daughter (Lakisha) started her own beauty shop called HAIR in the downtown area bringing in thousands of dollars. Somebody tried to rob them but ended up running butt naked down the street. That was the first and only robbery attempt. She made him strip and hit him with a belt. Even I had to laugh at that.

My other daughter (Andria) opened a shop across town called HAIR PIECES. She did that so that the two shops would not compete. They actually cornered the market and each ran four other salons out of business. So when they are not in the board room they are spewing their creative juices. It works for them.

Well I guess I will holla at ya'll later. I got records to produce and money to make. I will leave you with one thing. A piece of good advice … DON'T LET ANYONE STOP YOUR HUSTLE. Not even yourself. Get out of your own way. You will thank yourself for it later.

978-0-595-49730-0
0-595-49730-6